Praise for

High Marks for Murder

"Wonderful storytelling . . . A superb ghost story."
—Emily Brightwell

"An enjoyable mystery set in England's dynamic Edwardian period that is sure to please . . . The characters are intriguing, each with a hint of a tragic past."
—*The Romance Readers Connection*

"Very well done and definitely for those who like their mysteries on the lighter side."
—ReviewingTheEvidence.com

"School headmistress Meredith Llewellyn is bright and intuitive and the paranormal atmosphere adds an interesting touch." —*Romantic Times*

"Very atmospheric [with] a gothic feel . . . Readers will give high marks to Ms. Kent for an interesting, creative whodunit." —*Genre Go Round Reviews*

"A great cozy writer." —*Gumshoe Review*

D1010211

FINISHED OFF

Rebecca Kent

BERKLEY PRIME CRIME, NEW YORK

THE BERKLEY PUBLISHING GROUP
Published by the Penguin Group
Penguin Group (USA) Inc.
375 Hudson Street, New York, New York 10014, USA
Penguin Group (Canada), 90 Eglinton Avenue East, Suite 700, Toronto, Ontario M4P 2Y3, Canada
(a division of Pearson Penguin Canada Inc.)
Penguin Books Ltd., 80 Strand, London WC2R 0RL, England
Penguin Group Ireland, 25 St. Stephen's Green, Dublin 2, Ireland (a division of Penguin Books Ltd.)
Penguin Group (Australia), 250 Camberwell Road, Camberwell, Victoria 3124, Australia
(a division of Pearson Australia Group Pty. Ltd.)
Penguin Books India Pvt. Ltd., 11 Community Centre, Panchsheel Park, New Delhi—110 017, India
Penguin Group (NZ), 67 Apollo Drive, Rosedale, North Shore 0632, New Zealand
(a division of Pearson New Zealand Ltd.)
Penguin Books (South Africa) (Pty.) Ltd., 24 Sturdee Avenue, Rosebank, Johannesburg 2196,
South Africa

Penguin Books Ltd., Registered Offices: 80 Strand, London WC2R 0RL, England

This is a work of fiction. Names, characters, places, and incidents either are the product of the author's imagination or are used fictitiously, and any resemblance to actual persons, living or dead, business establishments, events, or locales is entirely coincidental. The publisher does not have any control over and does not assume any responsibility for author or third-party websites or their content.

FINISHED OFF

A Berkley Prime Crime Book / published by arrangement with the author

PRINTING HISTORY
Berkley Prime Crime mass-market edition / April 2009

Copyright © 2009 by Doreen Roberts Hight.
Interior text design by Kristin del Rosario.

ISBN: 978-0-425-22811-1

BERKLEY® PRIME CRIME
Berkley Prime Crime Books are published by The Berkley Publishing Group,
a division of Penguin Group (USA) Inc.,
375 Hudson Street, New York, New York 10014.
BERKLEY® PRIME CRIME and the PRIME CRIME logo are trademarks of Penguin Group (USA) Inc.

PRINTED IN THE UNITED STATES OF AMERICA

10 9 8 7 6 5 4 3 2 1

To Bill,
for making my life beautiful.

Acknowledgments

As always, I could not have written this book without the generous help and contribution of others.

First and foremost, my editor, Sandra Harding, who came up with the knockout title. I value your expertise, your great sense of story, your encouragement and enthusiasm, and most of all, your friendship. Thank you for making me look good.

My agent, Paige Wheeler. I truly appreciate your loyalty and respect for my work. It means a lot to me. Thank you.

My lifetime friend, Ann Wraight. Thanks for all the great research material. You inspire me.

Berkley's amazing art department. Every time I think they can't possibly come up with a better cover than the last, they prove me wrong. This is one standout cover and I thank you.

My mother, for instilling in me the importance of discipline, the value of hard work, and the wisdom to know when to quit.

My incredible fans. Thank you for taking the time to write and tell me that you enjoy my books. There can be no greater reward for a writer than that.

My husband, who puts up with me every day and still keeps his sense of humor.

Chapter 1

"You look pensive, Meredith. Is something troubling you?" Felicity Cross pulled a hairpin from her auburn hair and stuck it back into the tight coil at the nape of her neck. "You haven't said a word about rehearsals, and the choral recital is only a week away."

Meredith Llewellyn finished her row of purl stitches and laid the knitting needles on her lap. She had been debating whether or not to confide in her friend. Now that the opportunity had arisen, she was still uneasy about revealing her secret. "I have a lot on my mind," she said at last.

Felicity sniffed, and swiped a hand at her prominent nose. "Don't we all. We have barely begun the twentieth century and already rumors of another war are floating around. Compared to that, worrying about our petty little problems is somewhat self-indulgent in my opinion."

Meredith held her tongue with difficulty. Considering Felicity's vocation was instructing privileged young ladies in Romance languages and literature, the woman had an unfortunate way with words.

The other woman seated in the teacher's lounge, however, showed far more sympathy. Esmeralda Pickard leaned forward on her chair, her blue eyes filled with concern. "What is it, Meredith? It is not like you to be so reticent. I do hope your duties are not becoming too much for you. I cannot begin to imagine what Bellehaven House would be without its eminent head mistress."

Felicity snorted in a most unbecoming way. "The day Meredith steps down from her post will be the day the earth stands still."

Essie, as she was affectionately known, sat up straight. "Not everyone has your infinite energy, Felicity. Taking charge of a finishing school for young ladies must be an exhausting and arduous task. I know I should not do well at it at all. I find it tiring enough to teach the social graces. Sometimes it seems an impossible feat to accomplish. Especially when a good number of my pupils would prefer to be in London, smashing the windows of government buildings in protest for women's rights."

"Yet you always do well with your students." Meredith smiled at the young teacher. With her blond curls and baby face, Essie looked far too young to control a classroom of spirited young women, yet somehow she managed it with grace and efficiency. "They all adore you, Essie, and in spite of their idealism, I'm sure they secretly aspire to attain your elegance and poise."

Felicity snorted again. "Most of them don't even know the meaning of the words. As for breaking windows, I can think of far less beneficial ways to spend their time. Such as learning how to greet a member of royalty, for instance. How many of them will have that honor?"

Instead of taking offense, Essie let out a peal of laughter. "I think King Edward would enjoy meeting some of our spirited young women. They could certainly teach him a thing or two."

"Hmmph." Felicity lifted the cup from the saucer she was holding and took a sip of tea. "I think it more likely to be the other way around. He isn't known as the playboy prince without good reason."

"Felicity!" Meredith pretended to be shocked. She was

well used to her colleague's blunt tongue, and had long ago given up any thoughts of preventing the feisty woman from saying exactly what she thought. Even if it did offend whoever happened to be within earshot.

"You still haven't said what's bothering you." Felicity gave her a sharp glance. "Not under the weather, I trust?"

"I'm perfectly well, thank you." Meredith hesitated, glancing around the spacious room, even though she knew quite well she was alone with her two best friends. Sylvia Montrose, the fourth instructress at the renowned finishing school for young ladies, was at present on duty at the tennis courts overseeing the final tournament of the season.

"Then what is it?" Felicity leaned forward, a look of grim determination on her face. "Something has you in a snit. I can tell."

Meredith sighed. "I might have known I couldn't keep anything from you. The truth is . . ." She paused, even now reluctant to divulge what she knew was bound to cause a sensation. "I've seen another one," she finished in a rush.

Both women gaped at her—one with her teacup frozen in midair, the other with confusion written all over her flawless face.

Felicity was the first to speak. "I hope you don't mean what I think you mean."

Essie, who had not been blessed with Felicity's sharp mind, blinked. "What do you think she means?"

"A ghost," Meredith clarified. "I've seen another ghost."

"Heaven save us," Felicity muttered.

Essie merely gasped, apparently bereft of words. Not that Meredith could blame her. When Kathleen Duncan, her fellow tutor and friend, had first appeared as a ghost, even Meredith had trouble believing her own eyes. It had taken some time for her to realize that Kathleen wanted her to solve her recent murder.

She and Kathleen had shared many an adventure in their years at Bellehaven, but this was one escapade for which Meredith was ill-prepared, and it had been more by luck than judgment that she had discovered the culprit. Now it seemed, there was another ghost needing her help, and she wasn't at all certain she was up to the task.

"I didn't want to say anything at first." Needing to put her hands to use, Meredith picked up her knitting again. "I thought it might be my imagination. After all, one ghost in somebody's lifetime is quite enough."

"Apparently not for the ghosts." None too gently, Felicity replaced her cup in its saucer. "Word must have got around in the netherworld, or wherever it is ghosts congregate, that you are the great benefactor, the ghost savior, the sleuth who solves their murders. They're probably lining up right now, waiting for their turn to be avenged so they can float off in peace."

"I don't find that amusing, Felicity." Meredith raised her chin. Although Felicity had grudgingly accepted that she, Meredith, had on previous occasions encountered the ghost of her dear departed friend, the pragmatic teacher still viewed the entire episode with a certain lack of conviction.

"I'm not trying to be amusing." Felicity shook her head. "I'm being realistic. If you really did see another ghost, then obviously you have stirred up a nest of hornets in the ghost world. So what are you going to do about it?"

"I don't know." Meredith dropped her knitting again. "I would infinitely prefer to ignore her and hope she goes away, but she seems so helpless and pitiful. I feel obligated to help."

"Same old Meredith." Felicity shrugged. "No wonder people take advantage of you. Even dead people."

Essie found her voice, albeit a shade higher in octave. "You said 'she.' This ghost is a woman? Someone you know?" She coughed. "I mean knew."

Meredith shook her head. "This time it's a child. A little girl. I've never seen her before."

Even Felicity seemed startled by this revelation. "A *child*? Are you telling me a child was murdered?"

"Well, I don't know for certain, of course. The truth is,

Kathleen's ghost brought her to me, and since Kathleen had been murdered, I assume the child had been also."

"But you knew Kathleen before she was killed. We all did. After all, we worked with her for years. I can understand why her ghost would come to you for help." Felicity shook her head. "Listen to me. I can't believe I actually said that."

"Because you know it's true," Meredith said with a catch in her voice. Even now, she found it hard to speak of the beloved teacher and friend who had died so recently.

"But why would Kathleen bring you an unknown child?"

"I imagine Kathleen thought that since I helped find her murderer, I could do the same for the child."

"When was this?"

"A week ago. The last time I saw Kathleen's ghost. The child has returned twice since then."

"And just like Kathleen, she doesn't speak to you, I suppose."

"She keeps pointing at my chest." Meredith looked down at the knitting on her lap. "I'm afraid I'm not very good at this ghost business. Whatever powers I seem to have are unpredictable at best. I can't communicate with them, and they are barely in my vision long enough to understand what it is they are trying to tell me."

"Well, at least you can see them." Felicity slumped back on her chair. "It would help if you weren't the only one who can."

Essie shuddered. "Goodness, I'm thankful I can't see them. I should faint dead away, I'm sure."

Felicity rolled her eyes. "Well, be that as it may, if this is like the last time Meredith went hunting for a killer, it would seem we are in for yet another interesting adventure."

Meredith briefly closed her eyes. Much as she sympathized with the dead child, she wasn't at all sure she wanted to be involved with another murder. Especially of someone she had never been acquainted with and had no idea what had happened to her. "If only I knew what she was pointing at," she murmured.

She wasn't aware she had spoken aloud until Felicity spoke again. "I thought you said she was pointing at your chest." She stared at Meredith's bosom. "Perhaps it was something you were wearing. A brooch, or a pendant?"

Meredith sighed. "Not my chest, Felicity. I meant my chest of drawers. The one in my bedroom."

Essie giggled, while Felicity frowned. "Oh, well, that's different."

"Is it?" Meredith shook her head. "I still have no idea what she wanted."

"Maybe she wasn't pointing at the chest, but at something on it."

Meredith stared at her. "Now why didn't I think of that?"

Felicity leaned forward, apparently caught up in the puzzle. "Always assuming this ghost is real, and that you're convinced she is asking you to solve her murder, it might help to consider the possibility. What do you have on your chest that might be of interest to a child?"

Meredith thought for a moment, then her shoulders sagged. "I can't think of anything. I have a photograph taken with my late husband, rest his soul, and a little statuette standing next to it. Then I have an oil lamp and an alarm clock." She thought some more. "I think that's all . . . no, wait. My jewelry box."

Felicity's frown deepened. "You leave your jewelry out where everyone can see it? What if one of the maids decided to help themselves?"

Meredith puffed out her breath. "Really, Felicity, you must have more faith in our servants. Olivia and Grace have been with us for more than two years and have never once touched something that didn't belong to them."

"There's always a first time." Felicity held up her hands at Meredith's scowl. "All right. I'll give them the benefit of the doubt."

"What does the statuette look like?" Essie asked, surprising them both.

"It depicts a mother with her baby in her arms." Meredith caught her breath as the pain that never really left her sharpened. "My beloved Daniel presented it to me when we learned we were to have a child." She swallowed. "Shortly before he died fighting the Boers."

Essie uttered a cry of distress. "Oh, I'm so sorry, Meredith. I didn't mean . . ."

Meredith reached out to lay a hand on her arm. "It's quite all right, Essie. I have come to terms with his death and that of our unborn child."

"I don't know how anyone can accept the death of a child," Felicity said, her voice softening for once. "Unborn or not."

Meredith managed a smile. "Well, I really didn't have time to know him. But I do know what it is to lose a child, which is why I feel compelled to find out who this ghost is and what she wants from me. If I can bring some comfort to her grieving parents, then it is worth a little effort, don't you think?"

Essie hugged her clasped hands to her chest. "Oh, yes, Meredith. You absolutely must! We will help, won't we, Felicity?"

The other woman sighed. "I suppose, if you insist. Though I have to say, Meredith, I think you spend far too much time reading that silly magazine with all those dreadful detective stories in it. No wonder your head is full of murders and clues, and such."

As always, Meredith was quick to defend her favorite reading material. "As I've told you before, Felicity, the *Strand Magazine* is a respected periodical. The adventures of Sherlock Holmes are written by a renowned writer, Sir Arthur Conan Doyle, who was knighted for his work on the Boer War. His literary achievements are legendary."

"Yes, so you've said." Felicity sniffed. "I'm afraid, however, that I can never compare the tawdry prose of those ghastly tales to Shakespeare, Dickens, or Tolstoy."

Knowing she would never win that particular argument, Meredith murmured, "Well, to each his own. I do, however, thank you both for your support, in spite of your reservations. If I need your help with this little problem of mine, I will certainly let you know."

Essie nodded, though she looked a little worried. "I think I could manage a child ghost. Not quite as frightening as a grown-up one."

"Bosh." Felicity gave her a disparaging look. "One wisp of a ghostly presence and you'll be flat on your back."

"Well, it might not come to that." Meredith smiled at the young teacher. "If I can't understand what this ghost wants, she might very well give up and go away."

Felicity grunted. "For everyone's sake, let us hope she does."

The clanging of the school bell put an end to the conversation, much to Meredith's relief. She hadn't meant to bring up the subject of the ghost. It had been quite a shock to see the wispy form of the child standing in her bedroom.

She had thought that once she had solved Kathleen's murder, her association with ghosts would be at an end. It appeared she was mistaken.

Worse, she was afraid that Felicity's remarks, however frivolous they might have been, could very well come close to the truth, and that she was destined to be champion of a long line of ghosts that would haunt her forever. It was not a comforting thought.

Mrs. Wilkins pulled a batch of scones from the oven and set them on the kitchen table. The heavenly aroma of fresh-baked dough always made her ravenous, and a rumble in her stomach reminded her it had been several hours since she'd eaten.

She was tempted to pinch one of the scones to satisfy her hunger, but the sight of her two maids whispering together at the sink was enough to take away her appetite.

Whenever Olivia and Grace kept their voices that low, it was a sure sign they were up to something. Past experience had taught Mrs. Wilkins that meant trouble for her as well.

Having to cook for fifty young girls, as well as four teachers and varied staff, was a task that took all her energy and concentration. Being responsible for the antics of maids who didn't know the difference between suitable behavior and acting like street urchins was an added evil she could well do without.

Glaring at their backs, she demanded, "All right, you two, what in blue blazes are you up to now?"

The young girls sprang apart as if someone had lit a firecracker between them. Both of them turned innocent faces toward her.

Grace's soft, fair complexion contrasted vividly with Olivia's dark looks and determined mouth. When separated, Grace was easy to manage, putty in her hands. When she was in cahoots with Olivia, however, the two of them could be impossible.

Olivia, as always, took the lead. "Whatcha mean?" She tossed her head in defiance. "We ain't up to nothing, so there."

Knowing she would get little information from the belligerent ringleader of the two, Mrs. Wilkins turned to Grace.

The younger girl's pale, translucent cheeks tinged with pink as she stared at the cook. "It's nothing, really," she said, and immediately looked down at the floor.

"Nothing." Mrs. Wilkins crossed her arms over her ample bosom. "You're whispering about nothing. It didn't look like nothing to me."

Olivia made a sound of disgust in the back of her throat. "Can't two people have a private conversation around here without being cross-examined by the warden?"

Mrs. Wilkins felt her own cheeks warm with resentment. Although she was the last to admit it, she was really rather fond of the two girls. Having been separated from her own daughters, who lived in London and found the journey back and forth to the Cotswolds too arduous to consider paying their mother a visit now and then, Mrs. Wilkins had taken the maids under her wing as a surrogate mother.

The fact that the girls, and Olivia in particular, resented her motherly concern was of no consequence to the well-meaning cook. The girls were in her charge, and if she chose to make it personal, so be it. Though she had to admit, at times, they sorely tried her patience.

"Grace?" Mrs. Wilkins gave the girl a hard stare. "You tell me right now what it is you two are planning. That's if you still want to have supper this evening."

Olivia uttered a cry of protest. "You can't send us to bed without supper! I'll tell Mona."

Mrs. Wilkins raised her chin. "Miss Fingle to you, my girl. And the housekeeper's name is Monica, not Mona, as you well know."

"Yeah, well, if she didn't moan about everything under the sun, she wouldn't get called Mona, would she. Anyhow, she wouldn't want us to go to bed hungry."

"And you shan't, as long as you tell me what you two are whispering about." Once more Mrs. Wilkins glared at the other girl. "Grace?"

Grace glanced at Olivia, then murmured, "We was talking about the suffragettes."

Olivia turned on her. "Shut *up*, Grace."

Grace looked as if she were about to cry. "I hate going to bed hungry."

Mrs. Wilkins nodded at her. "Go on, Grace. What about the suffragettes?"

Grace turned beseeching eyes on Olivia.

For a moment the dark-haired maid scowled at her friend, then shrugged. "Oh, all right. It doesn't matter if you know, anyway. We joined the WSPU."

Mrs. Wilkins blinked. "The what?"

Olivia sighed. "The Women's Social and Political Union. We're members now."

"How can you join that? You're not eighteen yet."

"We lied about our age, didn't we."

"Oh, goodness gracious." Mrs. Wilkins covered her face with her hands. "This is going to be nothing but trouble. I can feel it." Secretly she had deep sympathy for the women's movement and their cause, but she'd heard enough about the sacrifices they made not to want her maids involved in their shenanigans.

"It's not going to make any difference to you." Olivia turned around and started running water into the sink. "Unless you want to join, too."

"No, I do not want to join. Nor do I want you two to join. Them suffragettes are dangerous, that's what they are."

"They are trying to get us the vote." Olivia spun around again, waving a wet hand at the cook. "That's why we want to help them. Every woman should be able to vote."

"You wouldn't know what to do with it if you had it!" Mrs. Wilkins was about to expound on why joining the movement was not a good idea when another voice from the doorway interrupted her.

"What in heaven's name is going on here? I can hear you all the way down the hallway." The tall, bony woman stepped into the kitchen, black eyes blazing. Her formidable jaw jutted out at a menacing angle as she demanded in harsh tones, "What is the meaning of this unladylike uproar?"

Mrs. Wilkins stared at the housekeeper in dismay. Miss Fingle was always looking for an excuse to chastise the maids. She felt it her duty to keep them under her thumb, and if they so much as attempted to wriggle out, she came down on them like the wrath of God.

Her punishments were harsh, and had lost Bellehaven many a good maid in the past. Mrs. Wilkins was of the opinion that they would all be a good deal better off if Miss Fingle were the one to depart, but since it was not her place to say so, she held her tongue on that subject.

Since neither Olivia nor Grace, however, seemed inclined to answer the irate housekeeper, it befell Mrs. Wilkins to speak up on this occasion. "We were having a friendly discussion, Miss Fingle," she said with a note of respect she certainly didn't feel. "I am very sorry if we disturbed you. I'll see that it doesn't happen again."

"Please do so." Miss Fingle sniffed, no doubt detecting the fragrance of newly baked scones. "In fact, it would be better to cut out conversation altogether while you are preparing the evening meal. After all, there can't possibly be anything of such importance to say that it can't wait until after supper."

"Yes, Miss Fingle." Mrs. Wilkins held her breath as the housekeeper's eagle stare roamed the kitchen in search of any minor infraction she could pounce upon as a parting comment.

Finding none, she sniffed again, sent a longing glance at the tray of scones, then swung through the door.

She could barely have moved out of earshot before Olivia exploded with laughter, echoed somewhat more hesitantly by Grace.

"'There can't possibly be anything of such importance to say,'" Olivia said, pitching her voice in a fair imitation of the housekeeper's gruff tones as she minced around the room.

Grace laughed with more conviction. "If she only knew."

Mrs. Wilkins stared at her, warning signals ringing in her ears. "If she only knew what?"

Grace slapped a hand over her mouth at Olivia's scowl.

"Nothing." Olivia hurried back to the sink. "She didn't mean nothing."

"Either you tell me right now, or no supper for either of you."

Olivia turned on her friend. "See what you've done?"

Grace cowered away from her. "I'm sorry. I didn't mean—"

Mrs. Wilkins took a threatening step toward Olivia. "Are you going to tell me or not?"

Olivia shrugged. "It's only that we're going into Witcheston next week for a meeting with Christabel Pankhurst, that's all."

Mrs. Wilkins let her mouth hang open for a second or two before she recovered her wits. "Pankhurst? Is she any relation to Emmeline Pankhurst?"

"Her daughter," Olivia said, her eyes shining in her sudden excitement. "Christabel is the daughter of the leader of the whole suffragette movement."

"Oh, my." Mrs. Wilkins covered her throat with her hand. "Better not let Miss Fingle hear about that, then."

"She won't if you don't tell her." Olivia gave the cook one of her rare smiles. "You won't tell her, will you, Wilky? There's a love."

In spite of her misgivings, Miss Wilkins melted. She sorely missed affection from her daughters, so every precious bit of warmth she could glean from the maids gave her immense satisfaction. "Well, all right, then. But you have to promise me faithfully that you will be careful. None of that talking back to the constables that got you into trouble the last time you went into Witcheston."

"Don't worry." Olivia grinned at her. "We'll be ever so careful, won't we, Grace."

Grace nodded.

"And," Olivia continued, "old Moaning Minnie won't ever know we was there."

"She'd better not. She'd have a pink fit if she knew you two were attending a suffragette meeting."

"Yes, she would," Grace agreed, "and I can just imagine what she'd say if she knew we've been ordered to break every window in the county council buildings."

Chapter 2

Meredith folded her hands on her desk and regarded the young woman seated opposite her. A rather prim woman, Sylvia Montrose was nonetheless quite attractive, her frail looks accentuated by her strawberry blond hair and green eyes.

Although adequately qualified, she had so far failed to gain the respect of her students, however, owing in some part to a slight lisp that gave them cause to make fun of her behind her back.

Meredith did not particularly care for Sylvia, though she wasn't sure of the reason. It could be that deep down she resented anyone attempting to take the place of Kathleen Duncan.

Sylvia had been hired to replace the dedicated teacher after Kathleen had met her unfortunate recent demise. Kathleen had been Meredith's right hand, assisting in duties that kept Bellehaven running smoothly.

While Sylvia's skills in teaching home management seemed sufficient, Meredith had been dismayed to discover that the new teacher had no concept of the work involved in the school's administration, and was therefore no help to her at all.

There was also the fact that Sylvia had been appointed by Stuart Hamilton, the charming and disturbingly handsome owner of Bellehaven House, without so much as consulting Meredith on her opinion. That had not sat well at all, and quite possibly had helped fuel Meredith's dislike of Hamilton's protégée.

Most of all, it was Sylvia's apparent inability to look anyone straight in the eye that irritated Meredith. Instead, the new teacher's gaze darted about, with a rather disdainful air that was at times quite insulting.

Meredith drew a deep breath, attempting to temper her rising resentment. "I was hoping you'd be able to assist me in taking care of the accounting." She pushed a pile of ledgers across the desk toward the other woman. "As you can see, there is quite a large amount of work involved, and I don't have the time to do it all."

Sylvia swept a glance across the ledgers. "Oh, I'm afraid I couldn't possibly. As I've told you, I have no experience at all with running a business."

Meredith smiled, though she felt more like frowning. "It's quite a similar operation to managing a home, actually, only more so."

Sylvia's gaze focused on her face for a second, then twitched away. "Mr. Hamilton made no mention of my having to attend to the school's business. I was under the impression I was hired to teach the students how to run their future households. Nothing more."

"Yes, well, I'm afraid Mr. Hamilton is quite unaware of the amount of work involved. Rather than inconvenience him, Miss Duncan offered to help me. I was hoping you would do the same."

"I'm sorry I can't be of assistance."

Sylvia's soft voice was hard to hear at times, her words made even more indistinct by the lisp. Even so, Meredith got the message. Sylvia was determined not to put herself out. Not even for her benefactor.

Meredith wondered what Hamilton would say to that. "Very well, I shall have to hire an assistant, I suppose. I just hope Mr. Hamilton is agreeable to that request."

Sylvia's fleeting glance clearly conveyed her disinterest in the issue. "If that will be all?" She rose, making the question moot. She barely waited for Meredith's nod before sweeping out of the room so swiftly she almost closed the door on her long skirts.

Meredith buried her chin in her hand and propped it up with her elbow. Whatever was Hamilton thinking, hiring someone as insipid as Sylvia Montrose to take over Kathleen's curriculum? Kathleen had been full of life, always reliable, and ever ready with a helping hand and an amusing comment to brighten the day.

Meredith sighed. How she missed her. In so many ways.

She looked up as the door opened once more, and Felicity stuck her head in the gap. "It's almost suppertime. What are you doing still working in your office?"

Meredith shook her head. "It's all this work. With Kathleen gone, it's steadily building and I just can't keep up with it."

"What about Miss Prissy? I thought she was supposed to help you." As usual, Felicity made no attempt to hide her contempt for the new teacher.

Meredith gave her a reproachful look. "Sylvia has no experience with business matters, and doesn't feel she can be of assistance."

"Bosh. Tell her she has to help or else she'll be sacked."

"To be perfectly honest, I'd rather not work too closely with her." Meredith got up and wandered over to the window. Her office overlooked the lawns, and at the far end in the gathering dusk she could see Tom Elliott, the aging gardener, and his assistant, Davie. They were raking up piles of golden brown leaves that had fallen from the poplars lining the driveway.

The signs of an approaching winter depressed Meredith even further. "I shall ask Mr. Hamilton if I can hire an assistant," she said when Felicity had failed to comment.

"Well, if he agrees, let's hope he allows you to do the

hiring." Felicity joined her at the window. "Or heaven knows what kind of assistant we'll end up with."

"If not, I suppose we shall just have to make the best of things."

"How are you coming along with the recital?"

Meredith welcomed Felicity's attempt to change the subject. "I shall know better at rehearsal tomorrow." She turned away from the window and smiled at her friend. "In the meantime, I feel quite hungry. It must be time for supper."

Following Felicity out of the door, she made an effort to dismiss the problems of the day. She had more than the management duties of Bellehaven to worry about. Foremost in her mind was the coming night, and the possibility of a visit with the ghost of a small child seeking justice.

"Absolutely not!" Mrs. Wilkins took a firm grasp of her rolling pin as if threatening to use it as a weapon. "No maids of mine are going to damage government buildings. I absolutely forbid it."

Olivia glared at Grace. "Can't keep your bloody mouth shut, can you."

"Sorry. It just sort of slipped out."

Olivia scowled at the cook. "Well, you can't stop us, anyway. What we do in our free time is our business."

"Not if it reflects on the school it's not." Mrs. Wilkins shuddered at the consequences of such a crime. "Imagine what would happen if some of them government officials found out two of our servants were breaking their windows. They'd shut down the school, that's what. Then we'd all be out of a home and a job. Is that what you want?"

Grace sent a nervous glance at Olivia. "Of course we don't, but—"

"No buts, my girl." Mrs. Wilkins brandished her rolling pin. "I'll box both your ears if I get so much as a hint that you're planning to do anything like that. Is that clear?"

"Yes, Mrs. Wilkins." Grace dropped her chin and stared at the floor.

The cook nodded. "Good." She looked at Olivia, and braced herself for another bout of arguments. "Olivia? Do I make myself clear?"

To her surprise, Olivia merely shrugged. "I s'pose."

"Then you promise me you won't go breaking no windows?"

"All right."

Mrs. Wilkins stared at the girl, wanting to believe her. "Good," she said at last. "I hope I can trust you both to keep that promise. Now, let's get this food into the dining hall before everybody starves in there."

Watching the two girls carefully as they loaded up the trays, she couldn't tell if they were really complying with her demands and forgetting any idea of sabotage, or if they were simply pretending to go along with her wishes.

She hoped and prayed it was the former. Whether the maids realized it or not, what she had told them was true. If they were caught doing damage to government buildings, there'd be hell to pay. For all of them. It could even mean the end for Bellehaven.

Even if the constabulary didn't shut the place down, who would want to send their daughters to a finishing school where the servants broke the law and quite possibly ended up in prison? It just didn't bear thinking about.

That night, Meredith had almost fallen asleep when the familiar chill crept across her bed—a breath of cold air that had nothing to do with the bite of the autumn wind outside. She knew immediately what it meant. A ghostly presence had invaded the room and needed her attention.

Heart thumping, she reached out until her fingers touched the oil lamp on her bedside table. Drawing it closer, she turned up the wick, then felt for the box of matches. Her fingers shook as she touched flame to wick, and soft light bathed the room.

Although she had tried to prepare herself, it was still a shock to see the misty outline of the child floating just a few feet away. Carefully, Meredith raised herself up until her back rested against the iron bars of the bedstead. "Hello," she said softly.

The child hovered a few inches above the floor. Slowly she raised one arm and pointed across the room.

Meredith frowned. Perhaps Felicity was right, and it was something on the chest of drawers that interested the ghost. "I don't understand what you mean. Are you pointing at the photograph?"

The child continued to point.

"The jewelry box?"

Still the child pointed.

Meredith let out a puff of air in frustration. "I wish I knew what it is you are trying to tell me."

Until that moment, she had not had a clear vision of the ghost, but as she finished speaking, the mist surrounding it seemed to clear. For an instant she glimpsed the sweet face of the child—light blue eyes, blond curls, and rosebud lips.

Struck by the beauty of the young face, Meredith felt a strong tug of compassion and sorrow. She stretched out a hand toward the child, but as she did so, the mist clouded up once more and swallowed the vision. Moments later, it vanished.

Shaken, Meredith got out of bed and reached for her shawl. The floorboards chilled her feet as she walked over to the chest. Once more she studied the photograph of herself with Daniel—he looked so handsome in his uniform. Raw pain caught her in the throat.

Carefully, she picked up the ivory statuette he'd given her. She heard again his voice, telling her that the model of mother and child had resembled how he'd envisioned her once the baby was born. Though the statuette was a constant reminder that she had lost their son, she still couldn't bear to part with the last gift Daniel had given her.

Even now, the wet tears clouded her eyes as she ran her fingers over its smooth surfaces. It was the shock and pain of Daniel's death that had caused her to lose her baby before he'd had a chance to draw breath.

She glanced across the room to where the ghost had hovered moments earlier. How the parents of that dear child must be suffering, having actually held her and watched her grow. That sweet face would haunt her forever, now that she'd seen it.

Even though the ghost had left, she hoped that somehow, somewhere, the child would hear her. "I will find out who you are, I promise," she said quietly. "I will do my best to find out who was responsible for hurting you and see that he is punished. But I'll need your help. I need you to give me a sign that will guide me on the right path."

She waited, fingers clenched, as the seconds ticked by. No cloud appeared, no ethereal mist, no shadowy figure of the child. Even the chill had left the room, and the air was still.

Aching with disappointment, Meredith climbed back into bed. She had given her promise and she was bound to keep it. She had set herself a monumental task, however, and one that seemed near impossible without the help of the child herself.

She lay awake for a long time. The little girl seemed so much more real to her now that she'd seen her face. How long ago had she died? Meredith didn't want to think about the manner in which she'd died.

When Kathleen had first appeared to her as a ghost, it had taken several visits before the teacher had actually conveyed the fact that she had been murdered and began giving her clues. Perhaps it would take time for the child to do the same.

She would just have to be patient. Not one of her virtues. But come what may, she would not rest until the killer was brought to justice. Perhaps then she could give some comfort to the parents, and allow the little girl to rest in peace.

The following morning Meredith had little time to dwell on her dilemma. She was late in arising, and had arrived in time for the morning assembly out of breath and out of sorts.

Assemblies were held in what had once served as a ballroom before Stuart Hamilton had bought the ancient mansion and turned it into a finishing school. All that remained of its former grandeur were two crystal chandeliers and the gorgeous pale blue carpeting on the balcony stairs.

The stage served as a platform for the instructresses while Meredith presented her morning address, for which this particular morning she was not fully prepared.

It didn't help matters when she saw Sylvia Montrose seated in the chair Kathleen had always occupied. Until now she had managed to keep the chair vacant, in memory of the late teacher.

Meredith's immediate thought was that Sylvia had sat there on purpose, to prove some ambivalent point. In the next instant she chided herself for her uncharitable conclusion. There was no reason why Sylvia should not sit in Kathleen's seat. After all, she was supposed to be there to take her place.

Even so, it rankled, and when the restless students took too long to settle down for the morning address, Meredith's rebuke was a little sharper than she'd intended.

She was quite thankful when she could dismiss them all and proceed to the dining hall. If she were fortunate, breakfast would improve her disposition and restore her good humor.

Felicity fell into step beside her as she marched down the long corridor to the dining hall. "You seem a bit liverish this morning," she said, keeping her voice low as they passed a group of chattering young women. "You must not have slept well."

"I slept too well." Meredith quickened her pace to keep up with her friend. Felicity always walked as if she were afraid to waste a single moment on such a mundane activity. "That was the problem. I overslept."

"Ah . . . then you must have been late in falling asleep."

Meredith glanced at her to find Felicity's keen gaze probing her face. "Yes," she said quietly. "I was."

"The ghost again, I suppose."

"Hush!" Meredith glanced around, relieved to see that everyone was out of earshot. "I must ask you not to mention it unless we are alone."

"Sorry." Felicity nodded with good humor. "So, did she tell you anything?"

Meredith sent her a suspicious look. She could never quite tell if Felicity really believed in her ghostly encounters or if her friend was merely humoring her. "No, nothing other than pointing at the chest again."

Felicity shook her head. "Frustrating. I don't know how you can put up with all that. I know I couldn't."

"I don't seem to have much choice." They reached the doors of the dining hall, where raised voices suggested most of the school was assembled. Felicity left to take her place at the head of one of the long tables, leaving Meredith to continue on to her own seat.

The smell of bacon stirred her appetite, and she filled her plate with sausage, bacon, scrambled eggs, fried tomatoes, and fried bread. The moment she picked up her knife and fork, however, she felt no desire to eat, and had to force the food down.

The students at her table were all in the choir, and were anxious to discuss the rehearsal that morning. Meredith answered their questions as best she could, but her mind was occupied with the sweet face of a child, and the lost look in her pale blue eyes.

By the time she arrived in the music room for rehearsal, Meredith felt a little more alert. The fifteen expectant faces turned toward her reminded her of her obligation—to present the best performance possible.

Pushing away her worries for the moment, she raised the lid of the piano and sat down. As always, the touch of the piano keys beneath her fingers soothed her, and as she played the opening introduction to Bach's beautiful composition, she began to lose herself in the music.

The voices soared in unison, producing a pleasant enough sound, though a little too unsynchronized for her satisfaction. She lifted her hands and waited for the voices to die away into silence.

Standing, she faced the girls. "That was very nice, ladies. The notes are on key, and now we just need to bring it in a little sharper. Like this." She opened her mouth and began singing, punching the air with an imaginary baton to emphasize the beat.

Meredith had always maintained that while she didn't have much of a voice, she did know how to emphasize in the right places. She was doing so with gusto when it occurred to her that her students' attention had wandered toward the door.

Even before she abruptly broke off, she had a sinking feeling about what to expect. As she dropped her hand to her side, a solitary pair of hands applauded her efforts. Unfortunately the sound originated not from the students but from the doorway.

"Bravo, Mrs. Llewellyn. A valiant effort, indeed."

Meredith turned to meet the amused gaze of Stuart Hamilton. Drat the man. He always seemed to appear at the worst possible moment. "Good morning, Mr. Hamilton." She resisted the urge to turn her back on him. "What can I do for you?"

"Not a thing, Mrs. Llewellyn. I happened to be walking past the door and heard your dulcet tones. I felt compelled to investigate the owner of such a . . . ah . . . unique voice."

Titters from the students raised the hairs on the back of Meredith's neck. Furious to feel her cheeks warming, she raised her chin. "Well, as you can see, I am quite occupied at the moment. I should, however, like to speak to you about an important matter. Perhaps you could meet me in my office in an hour?"

Hamilton raised a languid eyebrow. "An hour? I think I could manage that." He turned to face the girls and, much to their obvious delight, swept them an elaborate bow. "Ladies, I shall leave you to continue your delightful endeavors. I'm sure the end result will be quite spectacular."

Amid nervous giggles from the students, he turned back to Meredith and inclined his head. "Until later, madam." The door closed behind him, leaving Meredith breathless and bereft of words.

For the rest of the rehearsal she had trouble concentrating, hampered by the knowledge that at least half of her choir were convinced her assignation with the handsome owner of Bellehaven was of a personal nature.

The mere thought of that was enough to snatch any coherent thought right out of her mind, so she concentrated instead on the music. By the end of the session she was reasonably satisfied that with another rehearsal or two the Bellehaven choir would give a credible performance at the recital.

She dismissed the girls, aware of a hollow feeling in her stomach. Now she would have to deal with Stuart Hamilton again. Much as she hated to admit it, the man intimidated her on certain levels.

It wasn't just his impressive height, or his dark eyes that seemed able to seek out her most intimate thoughts, or even his resonant voice that seemed to echo deep inside her. It was more a matter of presence, an aura of control that seemed invincible and quite overpowering.

She'd had more than one battle of wits with the man, and had come off the worse for wear in most of them. She wasn't looking forward to the coming dispute, for she had no doubts that he would adamantly oppose her request for an assistant.

The matter would have to be handled with a certain amount of devious calculation. Fortunately she'd had plenty of practice.

Chapter 3

Meredith had barely settled herself behind her desk when a sharp rap on the door announced the gentleman's presence. Bracing herself, she waited just long enough to regain her composure before calling out, "Come in!"

He entered the room as he always did, with a long stride and a purposeful look about him, managing somehow to constrict the space between them as he sat down opposite her. Folding his hands across his chest, he murmured, "You wanted to discuss a problem, I believe?"

She rather resented his assumption that the important matter had to be a problem. "Not exactly. I wanted to talk to you about Miss Montrose."

"Ah." He regarded her with a thoughtful expression. "She is proving to be worthy, I trust?"

"In her duties as an instructress, yes. As far as one can tell in the short time she's spent here."

"Good." He waited, and when she didn't continue, he pursed his lips.

It was a habit that Meredith found most disconcerting, and she quickly looked down at her desk and began shuffling papers around.

After an awkward pause, he said quietly, "Is there something else concerning Miss Montrose?"

Meredith drew in a breath. "Yes, as a matter of fact, there is. As you may or may not know, the late Miss Duncan was a great help to me in matters of the school's administration. She was responsible for ordering supplies, both academic and domestic. She also arranged various school functions, such as garden fetes and recitals, and kept records of costs and funds raised."

A line of confusion creased Hamilton's brow. "Very admirable, I'm sure. You must miss her a great deal."

"I do, indeed." Meredith paused, then forced herself to look him in the eye. "I was hoping Miss Montrose would be able to help in a similar manner. Since you were so impressed with her qualifications when you hired her, I assumed she would be capable of the extra duties."

A gleam appeared in his dark eyes. "I see. I take it Miss Montrose is reluctant to cooperate."

"Reluctant, perhaps. *Incapable* is probably a better word. Miss Montrose informed me that she is unable to undertake the duties since she has no experience in these matters."

"Ah." Hamilton brought up his linked fingers to rest against his bottom lip.

For some reason Meredith had a great deal of trouble keeping her gaze away from the gesture. "I was wondering, in view of the oppressive amount of work involved in administration, if it would be possible to hire a full-time assistant." She paused, then added deliberately, "Or perhaps you would prefer to replace Miss Montrose with an instructress with more administrative capabilities?"

The gleam of amusement in his eyes disappeared. He lowered his hands and leaned forward. "That won't be necessary, Mrs. Llewellyn."

"Then can I presume that I will have the services of a full-time assistant?"

"Do you really need full-time help? Perhaps one or two days a week might suffice?"

Meredith met his gaze squarely, though her insides churned like an angry sea. "Hardly. In any case, I have found that applicants looking for a full-time position are usually more qualified than someone simply looking to fill in some spare time."

Hamilton stared at her for another long, painful moment, then his features softened into a rueful smile. "That's an excellent consideration, Mrs. Llewellyn. I bow to your judgment. You shall have your full-time assistant. I will see to it immediately."

Her surge of triumph was tempered by Hamilton's swift defense earlier of Sylvia Montrose, though she couldn't imagine why. "Thank you, Mr. Hamilton. I appreciate your understanding."

He rose, seeming to tower over her, and she quickly got to her feet. "Would you like me to interview the applicants, or will you be taking care of that?"

His glance rested briefly on her face. "I will see to it. I wouldn't want to encroach upon your valuable time. I'm sure you have quite enough to do as it is."

He bade her good day with a slight incline of his head, then crossed the room to the door. As he pulled it open, he turned back to her. "I'm gratified that Bellehaven House lies in such capable hands." With that, he gently closed the door behind him.

Meredith stared at the door, trying to decide if Stuart Hamilton's words were tinged with sarcasm, or if he'd really intended the compliment.

She sank down on her chair, and reached for her pen. It was a little disappointing that she would not have the opportunity to review the applicants, particularly since she would be working in close quarters with the new assistant. It would, however, save her a great deal of time, and she would simply have to trust Hamilton's judgment.

Seconds passed while she gazed at the door, a half smile on her face as she recalled their conversation. Then, annoyed that she had caught herself daydreaming, she dipped her pen into the inkwell, shook it on the blotter, and began to write her address for the following morning.

"How many times do I have to tell you we're supposed to keep our orders secret?" Olivia dragged the carpet sweeper along the upper hallway with little regard for how much dust she'd captured. "How long do you think them suffragettes will keep us in the WSPU if you go around tattling about their secret plans?"

Grace flipped a feather duster over a bust of William Shakespeare. "I didn't mean to."

"You never mean to." Olivia pushed the sweeper back and forth over a fragment of a white feather. "But you always do. Always. You'll get us shot, you will."

Grace looked up in alarm. She could never tell if Olivia was pulling her leg or not, and just to be safe, tended to take everything she said as gospel. "Shot? What for?"

"For telling secrets, that's what." Olivia frowned at her. "They're not just *our* secrets now, are they. These secrets belong to the WSPU, and if word got out what they was planning to do, the bobbies would be waiting for us. They'd drag us off to prison, and you know what that means."

Grace felt a cold hand clutch her heart. Mrs. Wilkins was always saying how dreadful things happened to suffragettes in prison, but she'd never exactly explained what those things were. Actually, not knowing made it seem all the more frightening.

Grace wasn't exactly sure that she wanted to know, but curiosity got the better of her. "No," she said in a hoarse whisper, "I don't know. What does it mean?"

Olivia sighed. "I'd better not tell you. You'll have nightmares." She started furiously pushing and pulling the sweeper back and forth over the feather, which remained stubbornly nestled in the carpet.

Grace felt sick at the thought of unimaginable horrors, but was compelled to pursue the matter now that she'd started. "No, I won't. Tell me what happens to the suffragettes in prison. I want to know."

"No, you don't." Olivia muttered something under her breath, then bent down and picked up the piece of feather.

"Yes, I do." Grace eyed her with suspicion. "You don't know, do you. You're just pretending you know. You don't know any more than I do."

"I do know, so there!" Olivia tucked the feather into her pocket and glared at her friend. "I know they go on starvation, and the prison guards make them eat."

Grace relaxed. That didn't sound so bad. After all, if the women were starving, they'd probably be glad to eat food. "Oh, is that all? Well, I wouldn't mind being in prison, then. It'd make a change to have prison food instead of the boring stuff Mrs. Wilkins serves up. And we could sit around all day and wouldn't have to work. We could talk to the other suffragettes and play tricks on the guards."

Olivia looked at her aghast. "What is the matter with you? You think it'd be fun to have a tube forced down your throat until you choked? Is that the way you want to eat?"

Grace stared at her in horror. "A tube? Down me throat?"

"A *big* tube." Olivia curled her thumb to meet her forefinger in a circle. "Bigger'n that."

"Blimey." Grace swallowed. "I dunno if I want to smash the town hall windows. What if we get caught?"

"We won't get caught." Olivia started sweeping again. "Besides, the town hall is only part of it. We have to set fire to a church as well."

"What?" Grace's shrill exclamation echoed down the hallway.

Olivia turned and slapped a hand over her mouth. "Shut *up*! Mona will hear you. We just got our days off back after the last time we got in trouble. If she takes them away again, we won't be able to follow our orders."

"And a bloody good job, too." Grace dug her fist into her hip. She rarely swore, but these were extenuating circumstances. "I am not going to burn down no church, so there."

Olivia gave her a look of pure contempt. "You are such a baby. You can't be a member of the WSPU unless you do your part in protesting."

"I'll find another way to protest. Like digging holes in the golf course. That's what some of the suffragettes are doing."

"Yeah, well, that's not our orders, is it. Our orders are to break windows and burn the church."

Grace lifted her chin. "I don't remember no orders to burn a church."

"That's because you were too busy talking to that big woman next to you. If you don't pay attention, you won't know what's going on."

"I'm not going to do it."

Olivia shrugged. "Suit yourself. I'll tell Miss Pankhurst that you are resigning from the WSPU." She picked up the sweeper and headed for the stairs. "There's plenty more loyal and brave women who will take your place."

Torn with indecision, Grace watched her start down the stairs. At that moment she really didn't care if she never saw another member of the WSPU. What she did care about was her friendship with Olivia. They were best friends. In fact, Olivia was the only real friend Grace had ever had.

She knew full well that if she didn't do what Olivia wanted, it would put a chink in their relationship. Knowing her friend, Olivia would take it as a personal affront. The gap would gradually widen to a chasm that could never be repaired.

But *burning a church*? That was sacrilege. It went against everything she believed in. On the other hand, the suffragettes were fighting for a good cause. Surely some honor could be found in the fight for women's rights?

Olivia had now turned the corner and was out of sight. Grace teetered on the edge of morality for several more seconds, then abandoning her principles, she raced for the stairs. "Wait, Olivia! I'll do it! I'll do it!" Praying that God would forgive her, she raced down the steps after her friend.

* * *

Meredith's favorite part of the day was late afternoon, when her classes were over and she could relax for
half an hour alone in the pleasant teacher's lounge.

Weak sunlight poured through the large window over-
looking lawns that swept down to a tangle of wildwood.
The shades of pink and rose in the room, picked out in the
curtains and carpet, always seemed to soothe and relax her.
It was a quiet time of day, and she looked forward to it.

Felicity's French class, Essie's lectures on etiquette, and
Sylvia's instruction on flower arrangements all ended later
than her own final class of the afternoon, leaving her time
to peruse the latest edition of the *Witcheston Post*.

The village of Crickling Green was far too small to
have its own newspaper, but often Witcheston's local news
included that rare occasion when the village had something worth writing about.

The circumstances surrounding Kathleen's death had
been deemed sensational enough to warrant a cover story
in the *Post*, much to the dismay of everyone involved.

Stuart Hamilton had gone so far as to protest to the edi-
tors, but by then, of course, it was too late. Bellehaven had
suffered a notoriety that would take some time to live
down.

Luckily, situated in the sleepy little village in the heart
of the Cotswolds, the school was fairly insulated from the
kind of exposure it might have had in national newspapers
had it resided in a town the size of Witcheston. Which was
good for teachers and students alike.

Settling herself down on her favorite brocade chair,
Meredith opened up the *Post*. Relieved to see no mention of
Bellehaven on the front page, she flipped it open to glance
through the other three pages.

She'd read somewhere that news ages fast, and that had
to be the case, since there was no mention of Kathleen, or
Bellehaven, anywhere on the pages. Sighing in relief, Meredith leaned back and began reading.

It was on the third page that she spotted it. Just a short paragraph or two about an orphanage near Witcheston, which had recently benefited from a wealthy landowner's will.

Intrigued by the generous gesture, Meredith scanned the lines. The orphanage was owned by the county, and the councilors would use the money to buy new beds and refurbish the kitchen.

There was a rather scratchy picture of the institution, and Meredith felt a pang of sorrow for the little ones incarcerated in that gloomy building. How sad. What a dismal start to a young life.

She gazed at the picture for a few moments, imagining mournful and hopeless children wandering the halls. It must be so miserable to work there.

How lucky she was, to work in this bright and beautiful mansion, with its gray walls reflecting the sunlight and its charming flower gardens that Kathleen had tended so diligently.

In spite of the tension she felt when meeting with Stuart Hamilton, she would be forever grateful that he had the vision to buy the home from its impoverished owner and turn it into the select institution it had become.

Bellehaven had earned a reputation among the more affluent members of London's society, and in spite of the unfortunate recent events, she and her fellow teachers would continue to educate and inform young ladies how to take their place among London's elite for many years to come. Smiling, Meredith returned to her reading.

She was deep in a story about suffragettes who had invaded a golf course and, using a trowel, had dug out the words *Votes for Women* across the middle of the eighteenth green, when Felicity barged through the door.

"I just cannot believe she would be that stupid," she declared, throwing the words over her shoulder to Essie, directly behind her.

"I'm so sorry, Felicity. I can imagine how terribly frustrating it can be."

Essie's soothing tones apparently had no effect on Felicity, who flung herself down on a chair with a low growl. "Drat the woman, that's what I say. Nincompoops like that should be banned from female company."

Meredith lowered her paper. "What has happened now?" She had not a single doubt as to whom Felicity referred. Her friend had clashed with Sylvia Montrose from the very beginning, and it seemed as though nothing would ever change Felicity's opinion of Stuart Hamilton's protégée.

"That Montrose woman, of course." Felicity raised a hand and gestured in midair. "I happened to pass her in the hallway just now. She was talking to a group of our students and telling them . . ." She paused, shaking her head as if she couldn't believe what she was about to say. "She actually told them that if they wanted a place in heaven, they will shun the women's movement and remain beholden to the men who will eventually provide for them. Ugh!"

Meredith sighed. "I suppose it's too much to hope that you didn't comment."

Felicity sat up straight. "Comment? Of course I commented! I told her she was completely archaic, both in her thinking and her teaching. I told her that the world is changing, and she had better get on the bandwagon or she'd end up a miserable, downtrodden slave to some arrogant brute who would make her do despicable things to earn her keep. That's if any man would be desperate enough to take on that harridan."

"Oh, Felicity." Meredith briefly covered her face with her hands.

"What?" Felicity sounded offended. "I didn't actually say the last part. Besides, I only told her the truth."

"In front of the students?"

Meredith's last hope was dashed when Felicity murmured, "They all applauded."

"You realize, of course, that she will go straight to Stuart Hamilton with this. She'll accuse you of undermining her authority."

"Poppycock."

"It's a legitimate charge, Felicity."

Meredith received the full force of Felicity's baleful glare. "I couldn't care less what Stuart Hamilton thinks. I'm within my right to state my opinion. I shall tell him so."

Knowing full well that it would be left to her to diffuse what could be a dangerous situation for her friend, Meredith sought to change the subject and pacify Felicity for the present.

"I read a story in the *Post* about the suffragettes." She handed the paper over to the still simmering teacher. "You'll most likely enjoy it. It's on page two."

She interpreted Essie's worried look and shook her head. All Felicity needed right now was a well-meaning lecture on tolerance from Essie. "I was also reading about an orphanage nearby," she said as Felicity took the paper from her. "Someone left them a great deal of money. It made me sad to think of those poor children, without a family to love them."

Felicity sniffed. "They're better off without family if their parents were anything like mine."

"It had an odd name." For a moment Meredith couldn't remember it, then it came to her. "Oh, yes, that was it. Chest House. Doesn't that sound utterly dismal? You'd think someone could conjure up a more cheerful name, like Rainbow House, or Sunrise Home, Pleasant Vista . . ." She smiled. "I think I'll write to them and suggest it."

Essie nodded in agreement. "Any of those would be better than Chest House. I wonder who thought that name would be good for an orphanage. How awful. Think of all those little boys and girls with sad eyes, desperately needing someone to love them. Why, it almost makes me want to cry."

There were actual tears on her long lashes, and Meredith felt sorry for upsetting her. She leaned forward to pat her hand, and as she did so, a vision of the child ghost popped into her mind. A little girl with sad eyes. Chest House.

She sat up, so suddenly Essie drew back, startled. "Good gracious, I wonder if that's what she meant!"

Essie's blue eyes regarded her in confusion. "If who meant what?"

Even Felicity lowered the paper and stared at her.

Meredith looked at each of them in turn. "My little ghost. She kept pointing at the chest. I wonder . . ."

"Oh, bosh, Meredith." Felicity rustled the paper and raised it again.

Essie kept on staring. "You think your ghost is someone from the orphanage?"

Meredith felt a twinge of excitement. "I don't know, Essie. But I certainly intend to find out. I shall go to this Chest House and make some inquiries."

"You're going to ask them if they sent you a ghost?"

Meredith winced at Felicity's bored tone. "No, of course not." She leaned back, her brow creasing in a frown. She would have to think of a way to ask about the little girl. Some way that wouldn't sound as if she were completely insane.

Perhaps she was being foolhardy, but this was the first glint of a clue to the child's identity. Something told her there could be a connection between her ghost and the orphanage, and in spite of what Felicity or anyone else thought, she would not leave that stone unturned.

Chapter 4

It was the following day before Meredith could pay a visit to the orphanage. Being a Saturday, breakfast was served an hour later than usual. Then she had to give individual permission to all the students who wished to go into the village that afternoon.

By the time she had finished the rest of her duties, she was in a fever of impatience to be on her way. She considered inviting either Essie or Felicity to go with her, then decided against it.

Inquiring about an orphan who might have died at the hands of a killer was likely to be a delicate matter. She didn't need Felicity's cynicism or Essie's squeamish disposition to hamper her efforts in finding out what she could about the child.

After ordering the maintenance man to bring around the carriage, Meredith pulled on her best navy wool coat and her favorite Sunday hat trimmed with blue and white silk blossoms. She wanted to look her best for the coming visit.

Reggie Tupper had been in charge of Bellehaven's maintenance since before Meredith had taken a position at

the school. As such, he often felt entitled to a certain de-
gree of familiarity with the staff, much to Felicity's wrath.

Although young in age, he had begun working at twelve
years old, and knew the mechanical aspects of the vast,
aging building better than anyone.

He also drove the carriage on the rare occasion that the
teachers ventured beyond the village. For the most part
Meredith put up with his impertinence, since he often
came in handy whenever brute strength was needed, and
he was usually most accommodating.

So when Reggie uttered a somewhat vulgar whistle at
the sight of her, she chose to view it as a compliment.

"Whew, m'm, look at you. Going to meet a fancy gentleman, are we?"

"No, we are not." Meredith gathered up her skirts and
stepped up into the carriage, ignoring Reggie's proffered
hand. "We are going to the Chest House orphanage, on the
road to Witcheston."

Reggie wrinkled his brow. "Orphanage?"

"Yes, I do believe I've seen it on passing. It's a large
house that's almost hidden behind overgrown trees and
shrubs. There's a rusty iron gate in front that leads up to
the road."

Reggie still looked puzzled. "Well, I reckon you'll have
to point it out to me when we get there." He closed the door
and climbed up on his perch.

Meredith settled back against the leather seat. Since she
didn't go out that often, she always enjoyed the ride to
town. Crickling Green looked its best this time of year,
when the leaves were on the turn and masses of daisies
studded the grasslands.

The steady clip-clop of Major's hooves lulled her into a
pleasant, restful state, and at times she was hard put not to
fall asleep.

The road wound up to the crest of the hills, and from
there she could see the honey-colored roofs of the village
cottages glowing in the sun. The road led them past the ancient church of St. Edmund's, where the staff and students

of Bellehaven worshipped every Sunday, and where dear
Kathleen had been laid to rest in the churchyard.

From there they traversed tree-lined hills and dales
bathed in the crimson, gold, and copper hues of autumn,
until finally the sharp, black and gray skyline of Witcheston
gradually surfaced from behind the grassy slopes.

They had almost passed the orphanage when Meredith
spied the rusty gate. Quickly she rapped on the window,
and had to do so several times before she caught Reggie's
attention.

He brought Major to a halt, climbed down, and opened
the door. "I can't see no orphanage, m'm."

"That's because we passed it." She looked anxiously
down the narrow lane at the thick hedges on either side.
"Can you turn the carriage around and go back?"

Reggie's laugh was short and incredulous. "Not blooming likely, m'm. There's barely enough room for me to
walk around here."

"Then I suppose we shall have to go to the next crossroads and turn around there."

"Right you are, m'm."

"Oh, and Reggie? The rusty gate I told you about. It's a
short way behind us. On the left."

"Yes, m'm."

"Actually it will be on the right when we come back."

"Yes, m'm. I could work that one out for meself."

Meredith twisted her mouth in a wry grimace as he shut
the door. There were times when she would like to box his
ears. Though she had to admit, the school would be in poor
shape were it not for Reggie's expertise. She shuddered to
think what her new assistant would be like. She would
probably have to lick her into shape before she got any real
help out of her.

It seemed a long way before they reached the crossroads, two miles from the city outskirts according to the
sign. Thank goodness they hadn't had to go into town before turning around.

She kept a sharp lookout on the way back, afraid to trust

Reggie and his wandering attention. He must have caught sight of the gate at the same time she did, however, since he pulled up just as she was reaching out to rap the window again.

Without waiting for him to attend to the door, she pushed it open herself and stepped down. He leapt down right in front of her, startling her into jumping back.

"I was about to open the door for you, m'm."

He sounded affronted, and anxious to make amends, she softened her tone. "I'm sorry, Reggie. I'm in a bit of a hurry. Would you mind waiting for me here? I shan't be long."

"Very well, m'm. I'll have a smoke while I'm waiting."

She nodded, and hurried over to the gate. As she did so, a shadow moved, close to the brick wall that surrounded the grounds of the orphanage.

At first she thought it might be sunlight playing tricks with her eyes as it filtered through the leafy branches of the elm trees. Then, just for a moment, she thought she saw the wispy shadow of a child, her blond hair gleaming in the rays of the sun.

Excitement gripped her and she started forward, but in an instant the vision vanished, and only the speckled silhouette of branches danced against the wall.

Had she imagined it, or had the child given her a sign that she had come to the right place? It had all happened so quickly it was hard to tell.

Anxious to get inside the orphanage now, she looked for a bell. There was no sign of one, however, and after a moment's hesitation, she laid a tentative hand on the gate and gave it a gentle push.

It creaked open with a loud groan, leaving a smear of rust on her white glove. Shuddering, she passed through and dutifully closed the gate behind her with her foot.

The bell, she discovered, hung over the massive door that guarded the entrance to the building. She pulled the bell rope, and heard the muffled echo of its mournful clanging inside.

She waited for some time before pulling the rope again, more forcefully and for a longer amount of time. Her reward came moments later with the grinding of heavy bolts being drawn back. The door swung open, to reveal a portly woman in a dull brown frock covered with a grubby apron.

Her tired eyes took in Meredith's appearance, and her bored expression changed to one of hopeful anticipation. "Yes, madam? What can I do for you?"

Meredith realized at once the reason for the woman's eagerness. Feeling guilty for raising false hopes in her, she said quietly, "My name is Mrs. Meredith Llewellyn. I've come to ask some questions about your orphans."

"You wanting to adopt?"

"I've been thinking about it, yes."

"Come in, come in!" She opened the door wider and Meredith stepped inside the dingy entrance, fervently hoping her lie justified the means.

"I'm Mrs. Philpot, the administrator of this establishment. Come with me." The woman led the way down a dark hall, dimly lit with flickering gas lamps on the wall. There were no windows to let in the light, and the place stank of antiseptic soap and stale cooking odors.

Mrs. Philpot paused in front of a door and pushed it open. "Please take a seat. I'll be with you in just a moment."

Reluctantly Meredith entered the office. The room was much smaller than her office in Bellehaven. A desk was crammed into one corner, and a tiny window afforded a view outside of unkempt bushes bordering a ragged lawn.

There were only two chairs, one behind the desk and one in front. Meredith brushed the seat with her gloved hand before seating herself.

Small piles of paper covered the desk. An inkwell sat on one corner and on the other corner perched a photograph of a group of children.

Eagerly, Meredith snatched up the tarnished silver frame and examined the picture. She studied each face carefully, both the boys and girls, but to her intense disappointment she didn't recognize the face of her ghost among them.

Replacing the photograph, she leaned her back against the chair. She must have imagined the vision outside after all. She knew quite well that her connection between the ghost and the orphanage had been flimsy at best. She had been so anxious to grasp any flicker of hope that presented itself, she had mistaken the reflection of sunlight for her ghost. If the photograph represented every child in Chest House, her ghost wasn't one of them. She would have to remove herself from this situation with as much grace as possible.

The door opened behind her and Mrs. Philpot bustled in. "Now then," she said as she lowered her formidable bulk onto the chair, "I'm quite sure we'll be able to find a suitable child for you to adopt. We have many lovely children here who will make excellent family members. Were you looking for a boy or a girl?"

Meredith thought fast. "A girl, most definitely. Actually, I have rather specific requirements for the daughter I have in mind. I shall quite understand if you are unable to fulfill them."

"Ah." The other woman's face clouded. "Then this isn't the first orphanage you have visited."

"Actually, it is the first." Meredith leaned forward. "The child I am looking for would have golden curls, the palest blue eyes, and she would be about ten years old."

"Hmmm." Mrs. Philpot leaned her hands on the table and stared at them. "That's a tall order. I don't know if we have a child like that." She looked up. "We do have a seven-year-old. Not exactly golden-haired, but a sort of light brown. I'm sure you would love her if you saw her."

"Thank you, but I don't think—"

Mrs. Philpot stood up, cutting off Meredith's words. "Why don't you come with me and take a look at our orphans. Sometimes we don't really know what we are looking for until we see it."

How true, Meredith thought. That didn't help her find her ghost, however. "I really don't think—"

Once more the administrator interrupted her. "Just a peek. It won't take a minute, and it would be a shame if you missed the perfect child because you didn't take the proper time to look."

Hearing the hint of reproval in her voice, Meredith rose. It would be best to humor the woman. She could easily say she didn't see what she wanted and leave. At least she would have satisfied the administrator.

Out in the hall once more, Meredith reminded herself that no matter how much she might pity these poor children, she could not take them all home with her. She would simply have to brace herself for the ordeal, and hope she could put those mournful little faces out of her mind once she had left.

The children were in the schoolroom, Mrs. Philpot informed her, as she led the way down the dismal corridor to a pair of double doors at the end.

Meredith could hear the childish voices, reciting words she couldn't quite catch. As the administrator opened the door, the words became audible. Guided by a thin woman with spectacles, the children were reciting a verse from *Alice's Adventures in Wonderland*.

Mrs. Philpot led the way to the front of the class, explaining to Meredith over her shoulder, "These are the older children, four years old and upward. The babies are in the nursery, but since you mentioned you wanted an older child, this is the best place to look."

Meredith was beginning to feel decidedly queasy. She had not thought all this through very carefully, and she now deeply regretted her rash decision to visit the orphanage.

She couldn't imagine what had possessed her to think that the vague and illusive gesturing of a ghost she still had trouble believing she could actually see could possibly lead her to this place. Her need to discover the identity of the dead child had addled her mind to the point where she was imagining things and grasping at straws.

Fragile straws at that. Now here she was, with dozens of eyes following her as she traipsed down the aisle, all praying that they would be the one to leave that dreadful place and find a new home.

How could she bring hope to these poor lost souls, only to snatch it away again? All on a ridiculous whim. How cruel. It would be many months, if ever, before she could forgive herself for this.

"Now, children," Mrs. Philpot announced, "this is Mrs. Llewellyn. I want each of you to stand up in turn, tell her your name and how old you are. Starting with you, Beth."

Miserably Meredith faced the children as, one by one, they stood and announced their names. Their clothes were ragged, their hair uncombed. Their ages ranged from about four to perhaps eleven, and although not one of them looked alike, they all shared the same haunted look in their eyes.

When they were finished, Meredith did her best to smile. "Thank you all very much. I enjoyed listening to your poem. I wish I could stay longer to hear more, but I'm afraid I have to leave." She hesitated, while the children stared at her with vacant expressions that gave no indication of what they might be thinking.

Unable to bear more, she nodded at the teacher, raised her hand in farewell, and quickly left the room.

Mrs. Philpot hurried after her, catching up with her halfway down the corridor. "I'm so sorry you didn't see what you wanted," she said, puffing as she struggled to keep up with Meredith's anxious stride. "Perhaps you could visit us again sometime. Most of the children who come in here are babies, though we do get older children from time to time."

Meredith made herself slow down. She reached the door and waited for the administrator to catch up with her. "I'm so sorry I wasted your time," she began, but Mrs. Philpot shook her head.

"Oh, no, I understand. You have a firm picture of what you want in your head, and nothing else will do. It's a shame. These children so badly want a home and a family to love them, but I do understand."

"Well, thank you again for your time." Meredith reached for the door to open it.

"Shame, really. I hesitated to mention this earlier, but just two months ago we had a little girl brought in who looked exactly like what you described. Nine years old, she was. Beautiful golden hair, blue eyes, the sweetest face you ever saw . . ." She shook her head, her words ending on a sigh.

Meredith froze, one hand on the door handle. Carefully she let go and turned to the woman. "Really? What happened to her?"

Mrs. Philpot shrugged. "Died, didn't she. Pneumonia, the doctor said. That's why I didn't say anything earlier. I didn't want to upset you."

"Pneumonia? Are you sure?"

The administrator frowned. "That's what the doctor said it was. She was ill for a while before that. Shock of losing her family brought it on, so they say."

Meredith let go of the handle. Reggie would have to wait a bit longer. "She lost her family? How dreadful!"

"It was dreadful, Mrs. Llewellyn. Poor little mite." Mrs. Philpot shook her head. "Lost her mother, her father, and her little brother. George Lewis was the manager of the Melrose Bank in Witcheston. They all lived in that big house on Meadow Lane, just as you're going into town. Lovely family. It was such an awful thing to happen."

"So what happened to them?"

"Well, as far as I know, they were all asleep when their bedroom caught fire in the middle of the night. Smoking a pipe in bed, they said her father was. Must have fallen asleep with it in his hand. They all died."

"And the little girl?"

"Emma was sleeping in another room. The noise must have woken her up. She climbed out the window. They found her stuck in the branches of a tree."

Meredith clenched her hands into fists. "Oh, the poor child."

"She didn't have no one to take her in, so they brought her here. Never spoke one word from that day on. Doctor said it was the shock. She caught a cold about a month ago. Died just last week, she did. Just about broke our hearts."

It couldn't be her ghost, Meredith thought, struggling against her rising hope. The child had died of a disease. She wasn't murdered after all. "How long ago did you say the fire happened?"

"Like I said, about two months ago. It was one of them warm nights with a dry wind. They said it spread really fast."

"I think I read about it. I seem to remember the child being found. Wasn't there a picture in the newspaper?"

Mrs. Philpot nodded. "It were all on the front page of the *Post*. Just a picture of the house burning, that's all. I do have a picture of the Lewis family, though. I kept it with Emma's things, just in case some long-lost relative comes along to claim them. Not that she had much, of course, other than the clothes on her back and a shabby teddy bear."

"Can I see the picture?"

In her eagerness, she had spoken without thinking. Mrs. Philpot stared at her as if she'd asked to borrow money. "You want to see a picture of the Lewis family?"

Meredith smiled. "It's not just morbid curiosity, I promise you. I'd like to see a picture of the little girl, just to see if she looks like the kind of child I have in mind. Then you will know what to look for in the future."

The administrator still looked doubtful, but after a moment's hesitation, she nodded. "Very well. It's in my office. Wait here and I'll fetch it."

"Thank you." Hardly able to contain her excitement, Meredith paced back and forth while she waited for Mrs. Philpot's return. Emma had to be her ghost. She had recently died and she sounded just like the image that appeared in her room at night. And yet, why would the child need her help if there was no murder to solve? What else could she need that Meredith could give her?

It seemed an eternity until she heard the administrator's heavy footsteps thumping along the hallway. A moment later she appeared, a crumpled photograph in her hand. "Here it is." She thrust it at Meredith. "It's a bit creased and all but you can see the faces."

Taking it from her with a hand that shook, Meredith studied the photograph. It had been taken in a spacious living room, tastefully furnished. The family stood in front of a huge marble fireplace, graced on either side by an elegant Queen Anne chair.

A small pendulum clock sat on the mantelpiece, just to the left of the woman's head, and to the right of the gentleman's head stood a pair of statuettes—rearing horses with their hooves pawing the air.

"It was taken the very day they all died," Mrs. Philpot said. "Can you believe that? The photographer brought it by here a week later. He'd heard about Emma and that she couldn't talk. He thought the picture might help her." She sighed. "Nothing could help that little girl speak again."

Barely paying attention to her, Meredith went on studying the picture. The woman held a baby in her arms, but it was on the little girl standing in front of her that Meredith focused. There wasn't a single doubt in her mind. The dead child, Emma Lewis, was indeed the ghost who had been visiting her.

"So, does she look like what you're looking for?"

Mrs. Philpot's voice made her jump. "Yes, yes, she does," Meredith murmured. She tore her gaze away from the photograph. "May I keep this? Just for a few days. I promise to bring it back to you." The other woman's puzzled frown prompted her to add, "I'd just like it to show to other orphanages so they know what kind of child I'm looking for, if that's permissible?"

Mrs. Philpot shrugged. "I s'pose it's all right. Just make sure you do bring it back."

"I promise." Tucking the photograph into her handbag, Meredith turned back to the door.

"I must say," Mrs. Philpot said, reaching around her to

open the door for her, "I never saw anyone so particular about the kind of child they want to adopt. You know, looks and age and everything. Pardon me for asking, but did you by any chance lose a child like that?"

Meredith stepped outside, gulping down welcome breaths of fresh, clean air. Turning to the administrator, she said quietly, "I did lose a child, yes."

It wasn't a lie, she assured herself, and if it would satisfy the woman, then she felt justified in misleading her.

Mrs. Philpot nodded, her face creased in sympathy. "I thought so. So sorry, dear. You can't replace them, though, you know. Even if you find a little girl who looks like yours, she won't be the same person."

"You're quite right. Thank you, Mrs. Philpot, for your time and for your advice. I'll certainly bear it in mind."

The administrator beamed. "My pleasure, Mrs. Llewellyn." She closed the door, leaving Meredith to descend the steps, her mind working feverishly on the question uppermost in her mind. What did Emma want, and how could she possibly help the child when she couldn't communicate with her?

Chapter 5

Much to Meredith's intense disappointment, the ghost failed to materialize over the weekend. She had hoped that her visit to the orphanage and the photograph would give her little visitor an incentive to return and help her understand what it was the child wanted.

By Monday morning, Meredith was beginning to worry that she would not see the ghost again, and never would find out why Kathleen had brought the child to her in the first place.

After giving her speech for morning assembly, she dismissed the pupils and ate a scant breakfast before proceeding to her classroom for the first lesson. Today her students were to paint a still life—a vase of chrysanthemums picked from the flowerbeds that morning.

The young women were restless after two days of relaxation, and she had trouble settling them down. It didn't help matters when a rap on the door interrupted her instructions on how to add depth to the painting to make it look more alive.

Meredith glanced at the door, her heart sinking when she saw Hamilton's profile through the glass. Drat the man. He could have chosen a better time to intrude on her schedule.

The students began tittering in expectation and Meredith gritted her teeth. Stuart Hamilton might well be the owner of Bellehaven, but she was headmistress of the school and had every right to dictate when he could have her undivided attention.

Raising her hand sharply, she indicated she wanted silence, then marched to the door and opened it.

"Ah, Mrs. Llewellyn! There you are!" He sounded surprised to see her, when it was perfectly obvious he had seen her at her desk through the window. "I want you to meet your new assistant."

Irritated, Meredith glanced at the person standing a few feet away from him, and stiffened. Great heavens! The man had brought her a male assistant. A young, attractive male at that. What was he thinking? She had enough problems keeping Reggie away from the girls. This was ridiculous.

"How do you do?" She gave the young man a stiff nod, then glared at Hamilton. "Mr. Hamilton, I am in the middle of instructing my class, and I won't be finished for another half hour. If you would kindly wait in my office with . . . er . . ." She glanced at the new assistant, who was gazing through the window of the classroom door as if he'd just sighted gold.

"Mr. Pratt," Hamilton provided.

"Hmmm?" The young man turned bedazzled brown eyes on Meredith. "Oh, no, actually it's Platt. Roger Platt. Pleased to meet you, I'm sure." He held out his hand, thought better of it, clicked his heels, and gave her a stiff bow.

"Military student," Hamilton explained. "Failed the medical tests. He's looking for a position as a teaching assistant."

"Really." Meredith gave the hapless young man a sour look then turned back to Hamilton. "I really don't have time to talk to you now. Half an hour? In my office."

A wave of giggles erupted from the classroom behind her. Turning, Meredith was incensed to see the front row of students all waving madly at the door, while Mr. Platt stood grinning and waving back.

Meredith directed her fiercest scowl at Hamilton's face.

"Oh! Right." He took the young man by the arm, preventing him from waving more. "Half an hour. Your office."

"Thank you." She closed the door with a loud snap and turned back to her class. "Ladies! A little more decorum, please. It is not in the least ladylike to flap your hand at young men. Or women for that matter. Most unbecoming. Kindly remember your station. Decorum at all times."

Several bored voices had chanted the last four words in chorus with her. Frowning, she turned back to her desk. Could she really be that predictable? She would have to take pains to curb that.

She had trouble concentrating on the rest of the lesson, which was rather obvious judging by the dismal efforts of her students. Some of the vases looked as if they would topple over any minute, while many of the chrysanthemum blossoms looked more like disfigured parasols.

Relieved when at last she could walk down the hallway toward her office, her nerves tightened when she saw Hamilton and his would-be assistant lounging against the wall outside.

They both straightened at the sight of her, and Hamilton had the audacity to grin at her as she paused in front of them.

He was wearing a bright peacock blue waistcoat under his dark blue suit coat, and a matching handkerchief peeked out from his chest pocket. With his hair combed back from his high forehead and thick black eyebrows dancing above his dark eyes, he looked roguish and devilishly handsome.

Aghast at her wayward thoughts, Meredith quickly unlocked her door and walked into her office. She immediately sat down behind her desk, bracing herself as Hamilton ushered in the nervous-looking Platt.

Waving at two vacant chairs, Meredith muttered, "Please take a seat."

Out of the corner of her eye she watched Hamilton flip his coattails and sprawl onto one of the chairs, stretching his long legs out in front of him. Hastily she averted her gaze to Roger Platt. He sat perched on the edge of his seat, turning his bowler hat over and over in his hands.

Ignoring Hamilton as best she could, Meredith stared Platt in the eye. "How much experience have you had?"

Platt looked confused. "In what, madam?"

"In the affairs of a finishing school," Meredith said with as much patience as she could muster. "Or any school for that matter."

"Well, actually, none, but—"

"I think you will find Mr. Pratt capable of attending to the duties you described to me earlier," Hamilton said smoothly.

Meredith turned a stern gaze on him. "It's not the duties I'm concerned about."

"Actually, it's Platt, not Pratt," the young man murmured.

Ignoring him, Hamilton pursed his lips, totally unsettling Meredith's insides. "Then, what are you concerned about, may I ask?"

Meredith could feel the dreaded warmth creeping across her cheeks. "It's . . . ah . . . Mr. Platt is of a rather tender age—"

"But exceptionally competent."

"Nevertheless, he . . ." She floundered for another second or two, then finished in a rush. "He'll be a distraction for the young ladies."

Hamilton raised both eyebrows. "I'm quite sure Mr. Pratt will conduct himself with the utmost restraint at all times."

"Yes, yes, of course!" Platt stuttered. "And it's *Platt*." He proceeded to spell it out. "P-L-A-T-T."

They might both be sure, Meredith thought grimly, but she certainly did not share their convictions. "I was rather hoping to have a female assistant," she said, giving Hamilton the sternest look she could manage. "In keeping with the rest of the faculty here at Bellehaven."

"Yes, well, we can't all have that which we prefer." Hamilton bent his knees and got to his feet. With supreme disregard for Roger Platt's sensitivities, he added, "We have to take what we can get. Pratt was the only one I interviewed with a glimmer of intelligence."

The young man looked somewhat put out. "Er . . . Platt?"

"There isn't exactly an abundance of qualified applicants desiring to work at a school for young ladies," Hamilton continued, showing no mercy.

Catching the sudden gleam in Platt's eye, Meredith had the distinct impression that the young man was extremely happy to be considered for the position.

She got to her feet, causing Platt to leap up from his chair. "Nevertheless, I should like to wait until a female applicant becomes available." She glanced at the young man, who stared back at her with beseeching eyes. "While I'm sure you would be more than adequate, Mr. Platt, I have my students to consider."

She transferred her gaze to Hamilton, whose expression had darkened considerably. Stuart Hamilton did not like to be opposed, and she had a sneaking hunch that being challenged by a woman only intensified his resentment. "I am quite prepared to shoulder the extra duties until a suitable applicant can be found."

"I simply cannot allow that." Hamilton took a step closer to her.

With the wall behind her, Meredith had nowhere to go. Feeling like a fox caught in a trap, she could only hold her gaze in defiance as Hamilton placed a hand on her desk and leaned in closer. "We cannot have our most valuable instructress overworked. Your classes will suffer. I must insist that you at least give Pratt a fair trial. Say a month or two? If there are any problems, you may report them directly to me."

Caught in his gaze, Meredith felt herself weakening. Hating herself for being so vulnerable in his presence, she muttered, "Very well. One month. At the slightest hint of a problem, however, you shall hear from me."

"I would expect nothing less." He kept looking at her for far too long to be comfortable. Just when she was about to suggest he leave, he drew back. "I'm so pleased we were able to settle this matter satisfactorily."

Seething inside, Meredith could do nothing but nod. He might be satisfied with the arrangement, but she was far from pleased. Platt had better be on his best behavior, or Stuart Hamilton would see a side of her he had never as yet witnessed.

She waited until he had left before turning to the fidgety young man. "Well, Mr. Platt. I suppose I should show you the duties you will be carrying out. You do understand, I hope, that the position involves no teaching whatsoever. It is a clerical position."

Platt nodded with enthusiasm. "Yes, yes, I understand, Mrs. Llewellyn. But Mr. Hamilton indicated that if I did well, I would be allowed to assist in teaching later on." Upon seeing Meredith's icy stare, he added hurriedly, "Once I've had a lot more experience, of course."

By that time, Meredith told herself, she'd be too old to teach and more than ready to retire. "You may hang your hat on the peg over there." She indicated the hat stand with a wave of her hand.

Platt hung his bowler next to her wide-brimmed hat, and then stood with an awkward stance in the middle of the room.

Meredith ignored him for a moment or two while she retrieved files from the cabinet and laid them on her desk. "You may work in here while I'm taking class or when I'm in the teacher's lounge. When I have duties to perform at my desk, I expect you to find other tasks to take up your time until the office is free. Is that understood?"

Platt nodded. "Yes, Mrs. Llewellyn."

"And this is mandatory." She fixed him with a forbidding look. "Stay away from my pupils. There is to be no contact whatsoever between you and the young ladies. Do I make myself clear?"

A little of the light went out of his eyes. "Yes, m'm. Perfectly clear."

"Then we understand each other." She proceeded to inform him of the general routines of the school, such as meal times, the hours she expected him to arrive and leave, and the areas of the school where he'd be permitted to visit.

"I assume you live in Crickling Green?" she asked as she opened the first file.

"Actually no. I have been living in Witcheston, but I managed to find a room at the Dog and Duck in the village."

She looked up. "You'll be living at the public house?"

"I hope that's all right?"

He seemed anxious and she began to feel just the tiniest bit sorry for him. Both she and Stuart Hamilton had been hard on him, without any real reason other than their own antagonism. "You have no family?"

He shook his head. "I grew up in an orphanage. I don't know my parents."

She caught her breath. "I'm so sorry. That must have been difficult." For a ridiculous moment she wondered if Emma had sent the young man to her for some reason, then immediately dismissed the idea. She was crediting her ghost with far more power than was possible. "It wasn't Chest House, by any chance, was it?"

He shook his head. "Harmony Home for Children. It's in Southfield, up north."

"Ah." She relaxed again. It would be best if she put Emma Lewis completely out of her mind. It was possible the ghost would fail to appear again, and even if it did, she had no idea how she could possibly help the little girl. The loss of the family was a tragedy, and she felt deeply sorry for little Emma for all she had suffered. She could only hope that the child could pass on and finally be at peace.

* * *

"So when are we supposed to go smashing windows?"
Grace asked as she followed Olivia down the narrow hallway to the dining room.

Olivia paused at the door, one hand on the doorknob.
"Tomorrow. We have to be at Witcheston town hall by
nine o'clock."

Grace almost dropped the tray she was holding. "That
late? It'll be gone midnight before we get back here."

Olivia rolled her eyes. "Not nine o'clock at night, you
silly cow. Nine o'clock in the morning."

Grace felt her stomach churn. "But it's not our afternoon off."

"I know that." Olivia turned the knob and walked into
the dining room.

"But we got into trouble last time for taking the whole
day off and on the wrong day as well."

"That's because you told Mrs. Wilkins where we were
going. If you hadn't said nothing, she wouldn't have known
we was gone and Mona wouldn't have found out about it
and took our days off away."

Grace felt like hitting her friend over the head with her
tray. "I think she might have had an inkling when we disappeared for the whole day and night."

"We could have lied. Just because she didn't see us
doesn't mean we weren't here."

Grace followed Olivia over to the first table and began
piling dirty dishes on the tray. "But we weren't here."

Olivia groaned and tilted her head back to stare at the
ceiling. "I know that and you know that, but she didn't
have to know that, did she."

"She would if she went looking for us."

Olivia glared at her. "Do you want to be a WSPU member or not?"

"Yes, but—"

"Are you prepared to carry out orders without question

as expected of you? Like you swore you would when you became a member?"

"Well, yes, but—"

"Then are you or are you not willing to go into Witcheston tomorrow to carry out those orders?"

Grace hesitated. "All right, yes, but—"

Olivia threw up her hands in exasperation. "But *what*?"

"I'm not setting fire to no church, so there."

"You've been *ordered* to burn it, so you'll have to follow orders."

Grace felt her lower lip trembling. "God will strike us down dead if we desecrate His house."

Olivia smacked a pile of dishes down on her tray so hard the top plate bounced. "Don't be daft. We're doing it for a good cause." She scowled at her friend. "We're helping to get equal rights for women. We're fighting the government so we can vote."

"I know all that." Grace shook her head. "But damaging a church, Livvie. That's really awful."

"Not when the Church of England is against everything we're fighting for, it's not."

Realizing she was getting nowhere, Grace tried another tactic. "How are we going to get there and back, anyway?"

"Same way we did before. We'll hitch a lift into town."

Grace let out a cry of protest. "I've still got bruises from the last time. Bumping around in that farmer's cart with all them smelly vegetables—it was horrid."

"Don't be such a baby." Olivia picked up the heavy tray and balanced it against her hip. "You're a suffragette now, Gracie. Brave, strong, and determined. Women's rights. That's what matters. Down with the government." She stomped out of the dining hall humming a marching song.

Grace picked up her own tray and followed her, reflecting gloomily that the last time someone thrust a placard in her hands that said "Down with the Government," she knocked over a policeman and had to run for her life.

She had a nasty feeling that this upcoming adventure was going to turn out every bit as badly as the last one.

Meredith woke up with a start, a thin sheen of cold sweat bathing her brow. She had been dreaming that she was trying to rescue Emma Lewis from a burning tree, and the flames were getting hotter and hotter.

She wasn't hot at all, though. There was a chill in the room, a deep penetrating chill that caused her entire body to shiver, in spite of the warm blankets covering her.

She sat up in bed, already anticipating the vision that hovered in the corner of the room. There it was, just a pale, green glow, no more than four feet high.

Fumbling for the matches, she found them and quickly struck one. Afraid that the ghost would vanish before she had a chance to talk to her, she reached for her oil lamp, almost knocking it over in her haste to get it lit.

At last the yellow light spilled across the room, turning the green glow into a soft white mist. In the center of it, the figure of the child ebbed and flowed, distinct for two or three seconds, before fading again.

Cursing her inability to hold the image steady, Meredith lifted the lamp to see her more clearly. "Hello, Emma. I'm really happy you came to see me again."

The mist moved, as if startled. For a brief moment the child's face looked out at her, streaked with tears, then melted away in the mist.

Alarmed, Meredith leaned forward. "Don't go! I need to know what you want from me. I can't help you unless you help me."

The mist dwindled to a mere puff of cloud, then expanded again. Once more the vision of the child appeared. An arm floated up, seemingly unattached from the body, and a child-ish finger pointed at the chest of drawers.

"I went there," Meredith said. "I went to Chest House. I learned about your family. I'm so sorry. But—"

She broke off as the finger jumped up and down in

agitation. Frowning, she stared at the chest. The child had to be pointing to something on it. Quickly she slipped out of bed, and barefoot, padded across the floor. Picking up the photograph, she held it out to the ghost, who had once more retreated inside the misty cloud. "Is this what you're pointing at?"

The mist faded a little. With a sense of desperation, Meredith snatched up the clock. "Is it this?"

The ethereal cloud dwindled even more.

Meredith pushed the clock to one side and took hold of her statuette. "This?"

She caught her breath as the cloud exploded with light. The child's face gazed out at her with such a beseeching look in the blue eyes that Meredith cried out in frustration. Then, in a flash of a second, she was gone.

With fingers that violently trembled, Meredith stood the statuette back on the chest. For several long moments she stared at the delicate figure of the mother clasping the tiny baby to her breast. Tears pricked her eyes. The poor child missed her mother. How dreadful that they hadn't been re-united in death.

Meredith caught her breath. Was that what the child wanted? To be reunited with her loved ones? Was that her mission? To bring them all together in death, as they had been in life?

But how was she to achieve this? She knew nothing about the world beyond the living. She had assumed that Kathleen had come to her as a ghost because she was trapped in the school grounds and Meredith was her closest friend.

But Kathleen had brought the child to her just before she had passed on. Surely she knew that Meredith wasn't capable of such an enormous task—to reunite a family separated by death?

Climbing back into bed, Meredith muttered aloud. "You expect too much of me, Kathleen. I have not the slightest idea how to go about such a quest."

She closed her eyes, making a determined effort to go

back to sleep. It was a long time, however, before she could let go of the guilt and frustration enough to drift into a doze.

She was dreaming. A burning house and she was inside. Searching for something, yet she had not the slightest idea what she was searching for or where to look.

Once more she jerked awake, to find the first fingers of daylight creeping across the sky. Then it came to her, what she must do. The dream. She had to search the house. Emma's house. The answer lay there. She had no idea where, only that it was there, and Emma wanted her to find it. With a renewed sense of hope, she scrambled out of bed.

Chapter 6

Grace huffed and puffed as she tramped along the wet road, trailing behind Olivia, whose brisk step had taken her several yards ahead.

The rain fell steadily, dripping off the brim of Grace's hat and soaking her gloves. Although she did her best to avoid the deeper puddles, the wet hem of her skirt flapped around her ankles, and her feet squelched inside her buttoned shoes. This, she thought sourly, was even worse than being jolted around in a smelly farmer's cart. Right now she'd gladly climb aboard anything that had a roof and a dry spot to sit.

Ahead of her, Olivia spun around and beckoned with an impatient arm. "Come on, droopy drawers. We'll never get there if you don't hurry up."

"We're not going to get there, anyway," Grace grumbled. "Not if we have to walk all the way."

"We won't have to walk all the way, silly." Olivia raised her hands to tighten the scarf she'd tied over her hat. "Once we get to the crossroads, there'll be farmers on the way to town. We'll get a lift, like we did last time."

"Last time it wasn't raining." Grace caught up with her friend and gave her a fierce glare.

"What's that got to do with it?" Olivia turned her back on her and continued marching forward. "We're suffragettes, aren't we? Forward and onward, no matter what stands in our way!" She raised a fist above her head and started humming.

Grace rolled her eyes. If she'd had any idea what she would have to suffer for the cause, she might have changed her mind about joining the WSPU.

Women's Social and Political Union. It should be called Women's Stupid Pranks Union. It wasn't going to get them anywhere. What was the use of smashing windows? Even if women got the vote, how would they know who to vote for? Everything that had to do with government was kept a big, dark secret.

So deep was she into her inner ranting, she failed to notice Olivia had stopped marching until she bumped into her.

"Ouch!" Olivia glared at her. "You trod on my toes."

"Sorry." Grace pulled off her wet glove and squeezed it to get some of the water out of it. "What'd you stop for, anyhow?"

"We're at the crossroads, aren't we." Olivia peered down the lane at the dripping hedges. "There's a tree down there. Let's stand underneath it while we wait for a farmer to come along."

Muttering under her breath, Grace followed her down the lane to the gnarled and twisted oak tree. It had lost most of its leaves, and provided little shelter from the rain.

Olivia leaned her back against the soaked trunk. "We shouldn't have to wait long."

"I hope not, or my hands are going to shrivel up." Grace hugged her own shoulders. "I hope Mona doesn't hear about this. She'll lock us up for a month if she finds out where we went."

"She won't find out if you don't tell her."

"Mrs. Wilkins will know we're gone."

"No, she won't. I told her we'd been ordered to clean out the attic. I told her it would most likely take us all day."

Grace shot her a look of grudging respect. "That was clever. But what if she goes up there?"

"She's not going up there, is she. With her creaking old bones, she'd never be able to climb those steep, narrow stairs."

"I hope not." Grace shivered. "I hate to think what trouble we'd be in if we got caught again."

"That's nothing to the trouble we'd be in if we got caught breaking windows. So you'd better pay attention and do everything you're told." Olivia shuffled through the wet leaves to get a better look down the lane. "Listen! I hear horses' hooves. Looks like our ride will be along any minute."

Even the thought of a dry place to sit did nothing to settle Grace's stomach. She was too busy worrying about what would happen to her if the bobbies caught them. The consequences were too dreadful to even think about.

As the plodding horse came into view, she thought very seriously about running off, back to the warmth and safety of Bellehaven. But Olivia had already hailed the farmer, and the cart was slowing down to a halt.

There was no turning back now. She was in this whether she liked it or not, and she would just have to hope that they could get through all this without ending up sitting in some cold, damp prison cell.

After announcing that she had errands to run, Meredith set off later that morning. Fortunately she had an hour or so before she had to be back in the classroom, and Reggie had assured her he knew where to find Meadow Lane.

With raindrops spattering on the window of the carriage, they jogged along the narrow lanes until Reggie pulled up at a crossroads.

Meredith waited while he climbed down from his perch and opened the door. "It's just a short walk from here, m'm," he said, holding out his hand to assist her. "I'll turn Major around and wait for you here."

She allowed him to take her arm as she stepped down onto the wet road. "Thank you, Reggie. I shan't be long."

He frowned down at her. "Want me to come with you, m'm?"

"Thank you, but no. I can manage quite well on my own."

He continued to scowl. "I know it's none of my business, m'm, but I do have to wonder why you want to go visiting a burnt-out house with nobody living in it."

Meredith nodded. "Quite right, Reggie. It is none of your business."

He shrugged. "Only asking, m'm, that's all. Just be careful in there, and give me a shout if you need me."

She glanced up at him. He wore no hat, and his fair hair hung in wet strands over his forehead. His limp mustache drooped over his chin and a rivulet of water ran down his nose and clung there for a second or two before falling to his chest. "You really need to cover your head when it rains." She wagged a finger at him. "You'll catch your death of cold running around like that."

"Nah, I'm used to it, aren't I." He shook his head, and drops of water flew off in all directions.

"Well, I insist that you wait inside the carriage until I return."

"Very well, m'm. Much obliged, I'm sure." He touched his forehead with his fingers.

She nodded, then left him to turn the carriage around as she hurried down the lane.

The house lay back from the road, with a driveway leading up to the main steps. Meredith paused when she caught sight of the ruined home. Part of the roof had burned away, and she could see the charred beams of what once must have been the main bedroom.

She could almost hear the screams from that poor child

as she watched her family burn to their death. How awful that they had no time to escape. That poor little baby who died with them. At least he was with them now in the hereafter, whereas poor little Emma still wandered alone, desperate to find her family again.

Once more Meredith was struck with the awesome task she'd been set. Somehow she had to find the answers in this house, because if not, she had no idea how to go about reuniting the child with her parents.

The front door stood slightly ajar, and swung open at her touch. The acrid smell of smoke poured out of the house to envelop her. It occurred to her that she could be treading on dangerous ground. There was no telling if the structure was unstable.

Stepping inside the hallway, Meredith felt an awful sense of abandonment. Water had heavily stained the carpet on the stairs, and the scorched banisters at the top leaned at a perilous angle overhanging the entrance below.

The stench of burning stung her nose and throat, and she left the front door wide open to allow clean air to enter. The walls had been stripped of paintings, and a broken chandelier swung in the light breeze drifting in from the doorway.

The first door on her right proved to be the living room. This room showed no devastation, though it had also been emptied out. The smoke had not reached here, and the wallpaper still clothed the room with its golden glow of swirling leaves and elegant tendrils.

In fact, apart from the fact that the room was devoid of furniture and drapes, standing in the center of the gold and green carpet, it was hard to imagine that anything untoward had happened to the lovely home.

Meredith stood for a long moment studying the room, without really knowing what she was looking for, or even why she had come. What could she possibly expect to find in this sad, deserted house that had once been a comfortable and sumptuous home?

"I need you to come here with me, Emma," she said

out loud. "I need you to tell me what to look for, what it is you want from here." She waited, willing the little ghost to appear, while the house creaked and groaned around her.

When it became apparent that Emma was not about to make an appearance, Meredith's disappointment was acute. She had mistaken her dream for a message from Emma. It had been just a dream after all. She should not have come.

She took one last look around the room, miserable in her failure to find anything that could help the little girl.

Retracing her steps to the hall, she glanced up the stairs. Emma's bedroom would be up there. She hesitated, re-membering the child's pleading face. What if the answer lay up there, in that bedroom? What if that was what Emma was trying to tell her?

Slowly Meredith walked to the foot of the stairs. Up there was where the worst of the fire had taken hold. It could be dangerous, with all the damage the house had sustained. Still, something urged her on. A child's face, pleading with her. Meredith placed one foot on the first stair.

For an instant she was tempted to shout for Reggie to continue the search for her, but thought better of it. There would be far too many explanations needed. Things she simply couldn't tell him. This was something she would have to do herself.

The higher she climbed the stairs, the stronger the smell of smoke became until she felt as if she would choke on it. Some of the floorboards on the landing were charred, and she carefully tested them with her foot before stepping gingerly over them.

Loud cracks and ominous creaking followed her down the landing to the first room. She opened the door and peeked inside. This must have been Emma's room. The once pink wallpaper covered in roses was now gray, with ugly black streaks where water had poured down the walls.

Staring at the soiled carpet, Meredith swallowed past

the lump in her throat. How terrified the child must have been to lose her ability to speak.

There was the window where she must have climbed out and into the tree outside. Moving about the room, Meredith tried not to think about that night as she walked over to the window. Again she felt a sense of despair. There was nothing in this room to help her. Nothing but the empty walls, and a lonely room bereft of a child's laughter.

Her heart heavy with sadness, Meredith left the room and closed the door behind her. She peeked inside four more rooms, all of which had been stripped of everything.

As she drew closer to what must be the main bedroom, the floor became more and more unstable. She moved carefully, aware of the growing danger, yet driven on by the conviction that somewhere in this house lay the answers she needed.

The blackened door to the bedroom was closed. She approached it warily, assuring herself that the bodies at least would have been removed. Even so, she had to steel herself as she pushed the door open and looked inside.

The roof was open to the sky, and rain dripped down the walls, soaking what was left of the royal blue carpet. Here the remains of furniture still lay, burned and scorched to an unrecognizable heap of ashes and debris.

A charred slipper lay by the door, and halfway across the room in the middle of the floor lay a baby's rattle, the paint scorched off it. The sight of that forlorn reminder of the little life that had been so tragically lost brought tears to Meredith's eyes.

She started forward with some vague intent to salvage the souvenir, but as she did so, the floorboards groaned and sagged beneath her feet. Shaken, she backed away to the door. Her foot struck something solid beneath the scattered remains of a once exquisite cradle.

She looked down, staring at the object lying at her feet and recognized it as the scorched and twisted statuette of a rearing horse. Some strange urge made her sweep it up, just as a shout rang through the house from below.

"Mrs. Llewellyn? Hello? Where are you? Are you all right?"

Slipping the horse inside her coat, Meredith fled from that dreadful room and its macabre memories. She reached the top of the stairs to find Reggie staring up at her, shock and dismay on his face.

"What the blooming heck are you doing up there, m'm? It's not safe, is it. The floor could cave in any minute."

"Do stop fussing, Reggie." Meredith started down the stairs. "I'm perfectly all right as you can see—" Her last word ended with a shriek as a loud crack interrupted her, and the banisters gave way under her hand. She stumbled, and pitched forward down the stairs.

"Look out!" Reggie leapt up the steps, both hands outstretched toward her.

Meredith tumbled toward him, smacked into him, and sent them both sprawling on the floor. Stunned, she struggled to clear her head before sitting up. Above her, the top part of the banisters hung over the side of the staircase while the lower half leaned at an angle.

Reggie lay facedown and at first she thought he was unconscious. He must have been only momentarily stunned, however, as he pulled himself up onto his hands and knees and gave her a dazed look. "You all right, m'm?"

Rubbing her ankle, she gave him a shaky smile. "I think so. And you?"

Reggie touched his forehead with wary fingers. "I conked me head on something but I don't think any bones are broken."

"I'm sorry, Reggie." She regarded him anxiously. "I certainly didn't mean for you to get hurt."

Holding the back of his head, he scrambled to his feet, then took hold of her arm to help her up. "What was you doing in here, anyway?"

"Just curiosity, that's all. I heard about the fire and came to take a look."

Reggie shook his head, then winced. "Ouch. Well, you know what they say about curiosity and the cat."

"Yes, I do." She hugged the horse beneath her coat closer to her. "I think I'll steer clear of burned houses from now on."

"Jolly good idea." He let go of her arm and walked over to the door. "I'd better go and see if Major is still there. I left him tied up to the signpost, but nobody can get past him unless they untie him and move him out of the way."

"Then let us go." She hurried after him, only too glad to be out of that house.

On the way back to the school, she drew the blackened horse out from her coat. Putting it on the seat beside her, she opened her handbag and withdrew the picture Mrs. Philpot had given her.

After studying it for a moment or two, she was satisfied. This was the same horse, one half of a pair, that had stood on the mantelpiece in the living room.

Frowning, she cast her mind back to her conversation with the administrator. *It was taken the very day they all died. The photographer brought it by here a week later.*

Both horses had been standing in their rightful place above the fireplace that day. Yet that night, one of them had found its way to the bedroom.

Meredith leaned back against the seat, allowing the steady rhythm of Major's hooves to relax her. What was it Sherlock Holmes had said? Something about an object being out of place. Look for something that was missing from its usual place, or something that was where it shouldn't be, and ask why.

Why, indeed. She didn't know the significance of the horse yet, but one thing she did know. It didn't belong on the floor of a burned-out bedroom. Someone must have put it there. Someone, perhaps, who didn't belong in that house? Was this what Emma was trying to tell her?

Somehow she had to communicate with the child, for something told her there could be a far more sinister story behind the tragic deaths of the Lewis family than anyone realized.

Chapter 7

The rain had stopped, but a cool wind continued to make Grace miserable as she stood on the corner of Witcheston's High Street. She and Olivia had barely reached the town hall before they were whisked off in the crowd to the main thoroughfares of the town, given placards, and ordered to march up and down while chanting slogans.

The heavy post kept slipping through her fingers, tearing her wet gloves until they were in shreds. Her arms ached from holding up the placard, her throat ached from shouting, and her stomach growled for want of sustenance.

Two hours they'd been tramping the streets, with no mention of when or if they were supposed to break windows. Grace was actually relieved on that point. At least the bobbies had left them alone, though two of them had strolled past fingering their truncheons and giving them warning looks.

Now all Grace wanted to do was go home. Back to Bellehaven, where dry clothes and a good meal were waiting for her. Even Olivia was dragging her feet, her shoulders hunched against the wind.

To make matters worse, they were just a few yards from a bakery, and the heavenly aroma of freshly baked bread tormented her empty stomach.

Deciding to take advantage of her friend's discomfort, Grace caught up with her. "I'm hungry."

"So am I." Olivia's pinched face turned in her direction. "Nobody said anything about eating, though."

"Well, they didn't say we couldn't." Grace rested her placard against her knees and dug in her pocket. "I've got a sixpence. Enough to buy a currant bun each."

Olivia lifted her chin and sniffed. "They do smell good." She looked down the street. "Go in there and get two of them. I'll hold your placard for you."

Grace didn't need asking twice. Abandoning her burden, she rushed down the street to the bakery, nearly knocking over an elderly woman in her haste to get inside the shop.

The sight of all the pastries and cakes made her feel faint. She just about snatched the bag of buns from the shopkeeper and fled out of the shop, back to Olivia, who had taken refuge in a shop doorway.

"Quick!" she said when Grace handed her the bag. "We've just got our orders. We're to go straight back to the town hall. They're going to start breaking the windows."

Grace immediately lost her appetite. "I'd rather stay here."

"You can't, can you." Olivia thrust her hand in the bag and withdrew a sticky bun. "Here, eat this. It will give you courage."

"It's going to take a lot more than a blinking bun," Grace muttered, but she took it anyway and stuffed it in her mouth. Chewing it down, she grabbed her placard, and followed Olivia around the corner and down the street to where a crowd of women had gathered outside the town hall.

"Look!" Olivia pointed a finger at the steps. "There's Christabel Pankhurst. Doesn't she look smashing?"

Grace went up on tiptoe to peer over the shoulder of the woman in front of her. The woman's wide-brimmed hat was adorned with huge ribbon bows and ostrich feathers, and seeing through all that clutter was a bit difficult.

She had just caught sight of a slim, dark-haired woman at the top of the stairs when everyone started chanting, "Votes for Women! Votes for Women!" The chanting got louder and louder, and Grace clutched hold of Olivia's arm with her free hand.

The voices sounded angry, and she could sense the hostility in the crowd. The women started pushing forward, and she tried to resist, but someone behind her gave her a hefty shove.

She stumbled, almost dropping the placard, and by the time she'd steadied herself, Olivia was nowhere to be seen. Frantically she stood on her toes, trying to see past the women in front. Everyone was pushing and shoving now, shouting in her ears, forcing her forward, closer and closer to the building.

"Olivia? *Olivia!*" Her voice rose in a scream but the harsh voices drowned out her desperate calls. She heard a tinkle of breaking glass, and a cheer went up from the front of the crowd.

The women behind her pushed harder and she struggled to stay on her feet, scared that if she fell, she'd be crushed beneath them. Closer and closer she stumbled, and now she could hear the crashing glass hitting the pavement.

The noise terrified her. Vivid images sprung to mind, of shards of glass flying through the air and slicing into her head and face. She plunged sideways, through a small gap in the crowd to her left. The heavy placard weighed her down and she let it fall, wincing as someone cursed heavily behind her.

Her terror gave her strength, and she fought her way out of the crowd. Stumbling at last onto a stretch of pavement free of the defiant women and the curious onlookers, she paused to catch her breath.

Tears ran down her face as she searched the seething mass of women for any sign of Olivia. She had to be in there somewhere, caught up in that awful riot.

Jumping up and down to gain enough height, she could see women throwing their placards into the windows of the town hall. Glass shattered and smashed to the ground all around them, yet they seemed unheeding of the dangers of the deadly flying fragments.

Then another commotion erupted from farther down the street. Male voices shouting, whistles blowing, horns trumpeting. The bobbies had arrived.

Screams arose from the crowd, shrieks of anger and pain. Grace could see the bobbies' truncheons flying, while women were dragged by their collars and thrust into a police-wagon.

She watched in horror as the door closed on a group of yelling, screaming women, then the wagon was pulled away and another took its place.

More onlookers had gathered now, pressing Grace off the pavement and into the street. Confused and frightened, she twisted this way and that, calling Olivia's name over and over.

She was on the point of giving up when she heard someone shriek her name. "Grace! Help me!"

She whirled around, facing the direction from where she'd heard that desperate shout. She was just in time to see Olivia bundled into a wagon and the door slam behind her.

The wagon moved off, taking her friend with it. At first all Grace could do was stand and stare after it, frozen with shock. Then suddenly, a surge of anger almost overwhelmed her.

How dare they manhandle her friend like that! How dare they treat her like a common street thief! Someone should teach them a little respect. Gritting her teeth, Grace clamped her hat more firmly on her head, then set off after the wagon.

Meredith arrived back at Bellehaven a little later than she'd intended, and she had to rush to change her wet clothes before heading for the music room.

As she reached the door, she could hear the students' voices raised in laughter. Apparently one of the girls was entertaining the others—and raising quite an uproar.

Curious to see who owned this remarkable talent, Meredith quickened her pace. As she drew closer to the door, however, she heard a male voice mingled with the girlish giggles and squeals. Setting her teeth, Meredith turned the handle and thrust the door open.

As she had expected, Roger Platt sat on the edge of her desk, surrounded by a bevy of giggling young maidens. One of them, Sadie Harcourt, was actually pressed against the young man's knees in a shocking display of familiarity. So intent were the pupils on attracting Mr. Platt's attention, they failed to notice Meredith until she raised her voice to be heard above the babble.

"Just *what* do you think you are doing?"

The young women closest to her sprang away and scrambled to the performance platform, leaving three of the students still engrossed in her new assistant's teasing comments.

"I think you should all let your hair down," Roger Platt said, actually reaching out to touch Sadie's bound locks. "It would make you look infinitely seductive."

Sadie simpered, while the other two girls gazed at her in envy.

Meredith took a deep breath and let it out slowly. "If any of you intend to enjoy your debut into society, I suggest you return to your places immediately." All three girls spun around and, amid giggles from the other students, dashed to join their companions.

Meredith turned to the young man, whose face now wore an anxious frown. "As for you, Mr. Platt, I will see you outside in the hallway. Right this minute."

"Er, right. Right away." He slipped off the desk and hurried from the room.

"Now then." Meredith faced the students and raised her hand. "You will begin singing your first aria. I shall listen to it outside, and if I hear one sour note, you will all return this evening for an extra rehearsal. Is that clear?"

A mumbled chorus of "Yes, miss" answered her.

"Very well, then. One . . . two . . . three . . ."

The pupils' voices soared, and Meredith left them to continue while she gave Roger Platt a piece of her mind.

When she stepped outside, he was lounging against the wall, hands tucked into the pockets of his trousers. As Meredith closed the door with a sharp snap, he pushed himself to attention. "Look, Mrs. Llewellyn—" he began, but she gave him no opportunity to continue.

"I warned you once," she said, putting as much disdain as she could into her tone. "Normally that would be enough. In deference to Mr. Hamilton and his somewhat biased opinion of you, however, I will give you an undeserved second chance."

Relief swept over Platt's face. "That's jolly decent of you, Mrs. Llewellyn, but—"

She held up her hand to silence him. "In the future, if I so much as see you within ten feet of one of my students, you will be instantly dismissed, and no amount of support from Mr. Hamilton will save your job. I hope I make myself clear."

He started to speak again, but once more she cut him off with a swift gesture. "Go back to your desk and finish those reports. I want them completed before you leave this afternoon."

A look of alarm leapt into his eyes. "This afternoon? I don't know if I can manage that—"

"You *will* manage that." She gave him her iciest stare. "You will not leave until they are finished."

He opened his mouth once more to protest, then apparently thought better of it and snapped his mouth shut.

Satisfied she had made her point, Meredith turned her back on him, opened the door, and walked into a chorus of a beautiful Bach aria.

Both Felicity and Essie expressed their admiration

when Meredith related the event to them later. Seated in the teacher's lounge, Essie clapped her hands. "Well done, Meredith! That must have put the young man in his place."

"I would have sacked him on the spot," Felicity said with a sniff. "Hamilton or no Hamilton."

"I think Mr. Platt was testing my authority," Meredith said, reaching for the latest copy of the *Post*. "Mr. Hamilton can be so overbearing and condescending, as if he has sole control over the management of Bellehaven. I believe Mr. Platt assumed he could do as he liked in Mr. Hamilton's absence."

"Well, I must say, you handled it well." Felicity picked up the book on Latin phrases she'd been studying for the past week. "I would have boxed his ears and sent him packing."

Essie giggled. "What's he like, anyway? Mr. Platt, I mean. I haven't seen him as yet."

Meredith wrinkled her brow. "A pleasant-enough young man, I suppose, even if he is somewhat misguided about his duties. He has no experience, so time will tell if he will be a valid assistant."

"That's what you get for allowing Hamilton to pick your staff. Look at the ignoramus he picked to replace Kathleen."

Unfortunately at that moment the door opened and Sylvia Montrose swept in. Judging by the outrage on her face, it seemed likely that she had overheard Felicity's comment.

Meredith dropped her newspaper and summoned a smile. "I'm so glad you could join us, Sylvia! We were just talking about the new assistant. Rather a dunce, I'm afraid. I'm hoping he will improve enough to be useful in the long run."

Sylvia flicked an uncertain glance at Felicity, then apparently decided to accept Meredith's version of the conversation. "I'm sorry he is causing you trouble. I haven't met him as yet."

"No, Meredith's keeping him all to herself." Felicity snapped her book shut and stood. "I haven't even seen him in the dining room yet."

"That's because he eats in my office." Meredith met her curious stare. "I don't want him mixing with the students."

"Ah, good idea." Felicity moved to the door. "Speaking of the dining room, isn't it about time we were in there?"

Glancing at the clock, Meredith quickly got to her feet. "I had no idea of the time. My little excursion this morning has quite disorganized my day."

Both Essie and Felicity looked at her. "You went out somewhere?"

Cursing herself for her slip of the tongue, she nodded. She had made the mistake of telling both her friends about her visit to the orphanage, and Felicity had beseeched her to forget about the little girl, since there was nothing she could do to help her.

She had gone so far as to say that she believed Meredith's encounters were actually apparitions that appeared to her in dreams, confirming Meredith's suspicions that Felicity never had believed that she could see ghosts.

Meredith had made up her mind after that to keep any matters concerning the ghost private, so that she couldn't be swayed by her friend's skepticism. It seemed, however, that now she would have to take both Felicity and Essie into her confidence after all.

Grace had to run really fast to keep the police wagon in sight, and by the time it reached the constabulary, her feet smarted from blisters and her lungs hurt to breathe.

Two of her hatpins had fallen out and were lying somewhere on the road behind her, leaving her hat to lurch from its sole anchor onto her shoulder. Fighting for breath, she leaned against the wall opposite the building where the bobbies were now hustling their prisoners through the doors.

So far she hadn't seen Olivia, so she had to be still in the wagon. There was only one bobby standing by it now, one hand holding the door shut while he waited for his companions to return.

Grace squared her shoulders and tried to ignore the collywobbles in her stomach. This was her best chance to get Olivia out of there and she had to take it now.

Opening her mouth, she let out a piercing scream. The bobby turned around, his truncheon at the ready.

Grace rushed toward him, still screaming, her hat flapping around on her shoulder like an aggravated parrot. "That man stole my handbag!" She pointed down the road at a group of pedestrians. "Look, there he is, in the middle of all those people."

The bobby stared at her for a second. "What's he look like?"

Grace started bawling as loud as she could. "He's young and he's got my handbag with all me money in his hand."

"Right. You stay there, miss, and I'll go after him."

The constable dashed off, and Grace didn't wait to see where he went. She tugged open the door and stared at half a dozen militant faces inside the wagon.

Olivia leapt forward with a cry of relief. "Grace! Thank goodness!"

"Come on!" Grace grabbed her hand and pulled her from the van. A lusty shout behind them warned her the constable was on his way back and wasn't terribly pleased to see his prisoners all leaping from the wagon.

The rest of the women split up in different directions. Grace plunged down an alleyway with Olivia right behind her, and the two of them didn't stop running until they were on the outskirts of the town.

Meredith waited until she was alone with Felicity and Essie that afternoon. Rather than risk having Sylvia walk in on her conversation, she'd asked them to join her for a stroll on the school grounds, something she often did when she had problems to sort out in her head.

She'd suggested meeting them in the memorial garden the students had planted in the woods in Kathleen's honor. The rain had stopped, and a weak sun peeked around the clouds. Standing by the flowerbed, she gazed at the students' handiwork. Dozens of golden marigolds nodded their heads in the afternoon breeze, while reddish-brown leaves fluttered down to join them.

Above her head, sparrows chirped in the leafy branches of the elms, and feathery ferns swayed back and forth beneath them. It was warm and peaceful in this little clearing. Meredith smiled. Kathleen would have been very happy to know she was being remembered in such serene surroundings.

She almost expected to see the misty shape of her friend appear, although she knew that wouldn't happen again. She couldn't help wondering if Kathleen knew of her struggles to help Emma Lewis. If so, she wouldn't be too happy with the little progress she'd made.

A rustling sound among the trees signaled the arrival of her friends, and she turned to greet them as they walked out into the small clearing.

Essie seemed nervous, and kept glancing over her shoulder, while Felicity seemed merely curious.

"It must be important if you're skulking around out here," Felicity said when she had reached Meredith's side. "You haven't been breaking the law, have you?"

Meredith laughed. "Nothing that I'm aware of, at least." She glanced at Essie. "You don't have to worry, Essie. Kathleen's ghost won't be coming back."

Essie rubbed her upper arms. "It's not Kathleen. I know she's gone. But what about your other ghost? The little girl?"

Meredith shook her head. "She only appears at night, and in my room. Nowhere else. Not even in the house she lived in."

Felicity gave her a sharp look. "You've been there? To that child's house?"

"Yes." Meredith walked over to the bench that Tom, the gardener, had placed by the flowerbed and sat down. "I went there earlier this morning."

Essie uttered a small sound of concern. "That must have been frightening."

Remembering her narrow escape on the staircase, Meredith gave her a rueful smile. "A little, perhaps. But I wanted to find out more about Emma Lewis."

Felicity shook her head. "I might have known you wouldn't give up. But if the child wasn't murdered, what does she want from you?"

"Well, as I told you, I thought at first it was simply to be reunited with her family." Meredith stretched her feet out in front of her. "But now I'm not so sure."

Essie came and sat down beside her, while Felicity perched a hip on the iron arm of the bench.

"So what are you saying?" Felicity demanded. "You're not suggesting the child was murdered after all?"

"No," Meredith said quietly. "But I do think it's entirely possible that her family was murdered."

Chapter 8

"Did you really think you could both be gone all day without me knowing it?" Mrs. Wilkins glared at each of the maids in turn.

Olivia stared back with her usual defiance, while Grace seemed to have acquired an intense interest in her shoes.

When neither girl answered, Mrs. Wilkins crossed her arms. "Miss Fingle wants to see you both in her office."

Grace whimpered, and even Olivia looked worried. "What for?"

"For taking the day off again." Mrs. Wilkins shook her head. In spite of her annoyance with the young girls, she prayed Mona wouldn't give them the sack. Maids were hard to find in a village the size of Crickling Green.

Most young women nowadays moved to London to be in service with affluent families who could afford to take good care of their servants. Grace and Olivia might not be the most industrious of maids, and they were certainly a handful from time to time, but she would really hate to see them leave.

Grace shuffled her foot back and forth, looking as if she would burst into tears any minute.

"We weren't gone all day," Olivia said, trying to sound a lot more defiant than she looked. "We came back this afternoon. We was up there cleaning out the attic, like we said, weren't we, Grace."

Grace nodded, her bottom lip firmly clamped between her teeth.

"No, you were not." Mrs. Wilkins puffed out her breath. "I went up there, didn't I. Miss Fingle told me she never gave you orders to clean it, so I went up to see what you were up to, and judging by the dust on the stairs, no one has been near the attic in months."

"We had to go to Witcheston," Grace burst out. "We got orders to go."

"Orders from who?"

Olivia nudged her friend with her elbow. "Shut your mouth, Grace."

"From the WSPU." Grace glanced at Olivia. "Sorry, Olivia, but we might as well tell the truth."

"I hope you weren't breaking any windows, like you promised." Mrs. Wilkins held her breath as the girls looked at each other.

"I never broke none," Grace said, her gaze fixed on her shoes. "I didn't see Olivia break none, neither."

"That's right," Olivia chimed in. "She didn't."

"Well, I suppose that's something to be thankful for." Mrs. Wilkins unfolded her arms and picked up her whisk. "You know these suffragettes are going to get you two into a lot of trouble one day, you mark my words. You'd best stay away from them, both of you. Stay out of trouble, or you'll end up losing your jobs, if you haven't already."

Grace whimpered again, while Olivia muttered something she didn't catch.

"Run along, then." Mrs. Wilkins reached for a bowl of eggs. "Miss Fingle is waiting to talk to you. You might as well get it over with."

Olivia marched to the door, while Grace lifted a tearful face and whispered, "Sorry, Mrs. Wilkins."

"So am I," the cook muttered. "Now get along with

you." She waited until the door had closed behind them before wiping away a stray tear. She was fond of the girls, and she hated to see them get into trouble. But they had to learn they couldn't break the rules whenever they felt like it.

Drat the suffragettes. Sometimes they were more trouble than they were worth. All that shouting and throwing things wasn't going to get them what they wanted. Women would always be downtrodden and mistreated by men. It was the way of the world, and more the pity for it.

Mrs. Wilkins heaved an almighty sigh, and went about beating her eggs.

"What gave you the idea they were murdered?" Felicity's frown was skeptical. "I thought you said that the father was smoking a pipe in bed and that caused the fire."

"That's what everyone thinks, apparently." Meredith shivered as the wind picked up and swirled the dead leaves around in the flowerbed. "But I found something I think might indicate something quite different happened." Quickly she told them about finding the horse in the bedroom.

Both women listened intently, but when Meredith paused, Essie shook her head in bewilderment.

"I don't see what the horse has to do with anything."

Meredith dug in her pocket and pulled out the photograph. "This was taken in the living room of the house,"

"You already showed it to us," Felicity said, taking the picture from her. "We've both seen it."

"Yes, I know. But really look at it. Look on the mantelpiece. What do you see?"

Frowning, Felicity stared at the photograph. Then her expression changed. "Oh, I see what you mean. There's two horses on there."

"Where? Let me see!" Essie took the photograph and looked at it. "Oh, I see them now." She wrinkled her brow. "What does that have to do with the one in the bedroom?"

Meredith reached for the picture. "It was one of the pair

on the mantelpiece. That picture was taken the day of the fire. I'd like to know how it ended up in the bedroom."

Felicity shrugged. "It could be the child was playing with it."

"I'm quite sure Emma would not have been allowed to play with a valuable statuette and leave it lying around. It's just odd, that's all. Something out of place that doesn't belong there."

Felicity shook her head. "I still can't believe you went all the way over there to look at that house. You really take this ghost business seriously, don't you."

"Yes, I do." Meredith tucked the picture back in her pocket. "So much so that I'm going to do some more investigating. I believe that Emma was trying to tell me her parents' death was not an accident. I think someone might have used that horse as a weapon to kill the Lewis family, then set the fire to cover up the murder."

Essie gasped in horror, while Felicity still looked as if she didn't believe a word of it. "Why would someone want to kill the entire family? Why didn't they kill the little girl as well?"

"Those are exactly the questions for which I have to find answers." Shivering again, Meredith stood. "Now that I have an assistant, such as he is, I have a little more time to do some investigating." She looked up at Felicity, then down at Essie's anxious face. "I may need your help in this at some time."

"Of course," Essie said at once. "I'll do anything I can to help." She glanced over her shoulder. "I just don't want to see any ghosts."

"Don't worry." Meredith drew her shawl closer about her shoulders. "It seems that I am the only one who can see them, anyway. Even I am unable to keep them here for long. As I've said before, whatever abilities I might have are somewhat limited."

Felicity grunted. "You never had any of these abilities until Kathleen died and supposedly came back to haunt you."

Meredith nodded. "Kathleen helped me discover I have the ability to communicate with ghosts. It just doesn't seem very strong, and now that she's gone, I'm afraid the power might disappear at any minute. That's why I have to find out what happened to the Lewis family as quickly as possible, before I lose contact with Emma."

"Well," Felicity said gruffly, "I suppose you can count on me to help."

Meredith smiled. "Thank you, Felicity. For now, all I need you to do is keep an eye on Roger Platt, and make sure he stays away from the students and gets on with his work. I'll fit everything in between classes, as much as I can, anyway."

Essie laid a delicate hand on her arm. "I wish I could take your classes for you, Meredith, but I'm afraid I know nothing about art or music."

"Me either," Felicity said, hunching her shoulders against the wind. "I'd never be able to lead your choral group. My singing sounds like an elderly horse with the croup."

Essie looked worried. "The recital is only three days away."

Meredith patted her hand. "Don't worry, my choir is ready, and I certainly won't forsake them. The recital will go on as planned."

"Oh, thank goodness. Everyone is counting on you, and I know how much you'd hate to let them down." Essie shuddered. "It's getting really cold."

"Then let's go back indoors. I just wanted to let you both know what I'm doing and why."

"I'm still not sure why," Felicity mumbled as she followed them out of the clearing, "but knowing you, I'm sure you have a good reason."

She did have a good reason, Meredith thought as she walked briskly back to the school. A little girl wanted to be reunited with her family. If she could find out what really happened that terrible night and bring it to light, she just might make that happen.

In doing so, she would reinforce the hope that she

would one day be reunited with her own dear husband and child—a hope she would cling to until the end of her days.

There seemed only one option at present, and that was to find out more about the Lewis family, and who might have wanted them dead. The first place would be the bank where George Lewis worked. She would go there the very next day.

Having made the decision, she looked forward eagerly to the night, when she might have an opportunity to communicate with Emma again.

She fell asleep, however, without seeing any sign of the ghost. The next morning she awoke with a firm resolve to discover without further ado as much as she could about the Lewis family.

Immediately after her class, she gave instructions to a rather despondent Roger Platt, and then summoned Reggie and ordered the carriage brought around to the gates.

"Where are we going, m'm?" he asked as she climbed up onto her seat.

"We are going into Witcheston. To the Melrose Bank. I believe it's in the High Street."

"Yes, m'm. I know where it is." Reggie gave her a sharp look. "You're doing a lot of running around lately, Mrs. Llewellyn, if you don't mind me saying so. Is everything all right? With the school, I mean?"

"Everything is fine, Reggie. I simply have some business at the bank, that's all." She settled herself more comfortably on the leather seat. "Now, can we go?"

"Oh, right, m'm. Right you are." Obviously still perturbed, he closed her door and jumped up onto his perch. The carriage jerked as Major moved forward, and Meredith leaned back, wondering how much longer she could keep her investigation a secret from her handyman.

He was obviously curious about her frequent trips of late, and rightly so. Until now the carriage had been used very little, since the teachers walked into the village and used the carriage only for the rare trip to Witcheston.

In fact, poor Major had probably been lulled into believing he was retired, and all this activity must be quite a shock for him. Feeling guilty, Meredith listened to the plodding hooves of the aging horse, and tried to console herself with the thought that perhaps Major was enjoying this break from routine. At least it wasn't raining, as it had been the day before.

Entering the crowded streets of Witcheston, Major had even more to contend with as he joined a stream of horses, carriages, bicycles, and the occasional motor car. Harassed pedestrians dodged between the traffic, seemingly taking their lives in their hands in order to cross the road.

The motor cars in particular made Meredith nervous. Not only did they move far too fast, at least twelve miles per hour so she'd been told, but all those abominable explosions emitting from them every now and again made her jump right out of her skin.

Major was decidedly skittish by the time they reached the bank, even rearing up at one point when a motor car made that dreadful bang right in front of him.

She scrambled down from the carriage the minute it halted, half afraid Major would bolt with her in it. "I'll try to be quick," she told Reggie, and hurried into the bank, where several customers stood patiently waiting at the counter.

After a few minutes' wait, she reached the bespectacled young man behind the bars. "I'm Mrs. Llewellyn," she announced when the gentleman smiled at her. "I'm the head mistress of Bellehaven Finishing School in Crickling Green and I should like to speak to the manager."

The young man looked impressed. "Just one moment, madam." He hurried away and shortly after returned with a portly gentleman, whose waistcoat seemed in immediate danger of popping its buttons.

"This is Mr. Clark, madam," the clerk announced, then introduced her to the manager.

"Howard Clark, madam, at your service." The manager gestured to the end of the counter. "If you would care to step this way?"

Aware of curious glances from the other customers, Meredith scurried to the end of the counter, where Howard Clark waited for her.

"My office is down here, Mrs. Llewellyn." He led her down a small corridor and opened a door at the end.

Walking into the spacious room, Meredith gazed in admiration at the gold damask curtains with their gold filigree rods, the shiny cherrywood file cabinets, and the magnificent gleaming oak desk sitting in the middle of the window.

"Do take a seat, Mrs. Llewellyn." Clark gestured at the chair across the room.

With her feet sinking into the deep burgundy and gold carpet, she crossed the room and sat on the velvet padded seat. She felt a little out of her depth. Not a feeling to which she was accustomed.

"Now then." Clark sat down behind the desk and rubbed his hands together. "What can I do for you today? You wish to open a bank account? Secure a loan? Rent a strong-box?"

Meredith smiled. "None of those things, Mr. Clark. I wanted to talk to you about the late manager of this bank. Mr. George Lewis. I understand he is now deceased."

The bank manager stared at her for a moment. "You were well acquainted with Mr. Lewis?"

"Not exactly, no." She paused, then added, "I have been in close contact with a member of the family, however. For reasons I am not at liberty to divulge, I should like to know more about the gentleman."

"I see." A frown creased Clark's forehead. "Well, I'm sorry to have to tell you that Mr. Lewis is in disgrace with this institution. I'm not sure I should reveal the cause."

Meredith caught her breath. She leaned forward. "Mr. Clark, I can assure you that no word of what you tell me will be repeated outside these walls."

Clark smoothed his hand up his forehead, as if brushing the hair away from his eyebrows. He must at one time have had a full head of hair, but all that remained of it now was a thick fringe of gray circling the base of his skull.

He had a habit of squinting, as if short of sight yet too vain to wear spectacles. He squinted at her now, obvious reluctance in every line of his face. "That's as it may be, madam, but—"

"Mr. Clark. It is vital that I have more information about Mr. Lewis and his family. I hesitate to go to the constabulary, but—"

"That won't be necessary, Mrs. Llewellyn." Clark uttered a nervous laugh. "No need to trouble the constables for such a slight reason. I'll be happy to tell you everything I know about the family, which isn't much, since I didn't have the pleasure of making the acquaintance of any of them except for George Lewis."

Meredith sat back, pleased that her mention of the constables had worked. She felt quite sure that Howard Clark had already had more than enough dealings with the constabulary, considering the manner in which George Lewis had died. The presence of constables couldn't have been good business for a bank.

"Thank you, Mr. Clark. Perhaps you could begin by telling me why Mr. Lewis was in disgrace."

Clark drummed the desk with his fingers for a moment or two, then said in a voice devoid of emotion, "On the day after Mr. Lewis died, I made the discovery that he had been embezzling funds from this bank."

Meredith took a moment to find her voice. "Mr. Lewis was *embezzling*?"

"Yes." Clark leaned back and laced his fingers together, resting them on his stomach. "It was a great shock to me, as you can imagine. I had always respected and looked up to Mr. Lewis. The night that he died I had left the bank earlier that afternoon for a meeting at our main branch in London. I returned by the afternoon train the following day to be met by a constable, who gave me the tragic news that the Lewis family had perished in a house fire."

He paused to wipe his brow, and Meredith felt sympathy for the man. He was obviously very shaken by his employer's death. "That must have been very upsetting," she said quietly.

"It was. Most upsetting." Clark drew a deep breath. "Anyway, as assistant manager, it was left to me to take over his duties. It didn't take very long to uncover the discrepancies in his records. Mr. Lewis had embezzled a considerable amount of funds and deposited them in his own account."

"I see." Meredith took a moment to digest this news. "How well did you know Mr. Lewis, outside of the bank, I mean?"

"I knew very little about his personal life, save that he had a wife and two children." Clark clicked his fingers. "Oh, and a brother. Maybe he can tell you whatever it is you want to know. He and his wife live at the other end of Witcheston, in a flat over Spicers, the ironmongers. I don't think they had much to do with each other. George Lewis spent most of his time with his own family, from what I heard."

Meredith stared at him. "Mr. Lewis had a brother? I was under the impression there was no other family."

The manager shrugged. "As I said, they didn't have much to do with each other."

Meredith had to wonder why Emma's uncle hadn't offered to give her a home. "This is all such a tragedy." She sighed. "A whole family gone . . . that little baby . . . such a terrible way to die."

"Yes, well, I'm afraid I can't help you any further." Clark leapt to his feet, startling her. "I'm a very busy man, Mrs. Llewellyn, as I'm sure you can appreciate."

"Oh, yes, of course." Feeling somewhat belittled, Meredith hastily rose to her feet. "I shan't trouble you any further. Thank you for your time."

His tone still curt, he showed her to the door. "Not at all. I wish I could say it was a pleasure, but frankly, any conversation about that man is quite disturbing."

Bidding him good day, Meredith left the office and made her way out of the bank. Deep in thought, she paused on the pavement, trying to come to terms with what she'd heard. George Lewis was an embezzler. It must have been kept quiet, since Mrs. Philpot hadn't mentioned it.

She thought about the elegant house that had been so cruelly damaged by the fire. It seemed the Lewis family had a comfortable living. Why would George Lewis find it necessary to embezzle money? Gambling losses, which he'd tried to hide from his wife? A business failure of some kind? Had he been paying someone to keep quiet about something he didn't want revealed?

So many possibilities, always assuming that the fire was not an accident and the family had been killed by someone, which was pure conjecture at this point since she really didn't know for sure.

If it wasn't for Emma, she'd just let it all slide. After all, if George Lewis was the kind of man who stole money for whatever reason, maybe it was just as well the child would not be spending eternity in his company.

Then again, she only had to think about Emma's beseeching eyes and she knew she had to pursue this thing to the bitter end. Or at least explore every possibility until she knew for certain what it was Emma was trying to tell her.

Chapter 9

"There you are, m'm." Reggie suddenly appeared in front of Meredith, cap in hand. "I had to take Major around the town. He got a little skittish standing at the curb here." Reggie winced as a motor car backfired in his ear.

So absorbed had she been with her thoughts, Meredith hadn't even noticed the carriage wasn't waiting for her outside the bank. "Where is he? Where did you leave the carriage?"

"Don't worry, m'm. Major's safe as houses, tied up in the courtyard of the Pig and Whistle."

She frowned. "I assume that's a public house."

"Yes, m'm. I'd suggest you join me in the ladies' lounge for a pint, but it's a bit rowdy right now. I don't think it'd be your cup of tea."

"Quite right, Reggie." She tilted her head to one side. "Do they have food at this Pig and . . . what was it?"

"Whistle, m'm." He pursed his lips and whistled a few notes. "Nice place." He looked more closely at her. "You peckish, m'm? They do have tables outside if you want a bite to eat." He glanced up at the sky. "Bit nippy with that wind and all, but it's sheltered in the beer garden."

"Well, since we'll both miss the midday meal at Belle-haven, I think a sandwich and a glass of cider would be very nice."

"Right you are, m'm." Reggie grinned at her. "Right this way."

She trotted to keep up with him as he led the way down several streets until they had left the hustle and bustle of the town behind.

"There it is, m'm." Reggie pointed ahead to the heavily beamed walls of the pub looming above the hedges. "The Pig and Whistle. Built two hundred years ago, so they say."

"Really." Meredith paused in front of the sturdy building to catch her breath. Tobacco smoke poured from the lower windows and was immediately snatched away by the wind. The babel of raucous voices inside convinced her to brave the chill and sit out in the beer garden to eat her sandwich.

Reggie escorted her to one of the tables, over which a red and white striped umbrella shaded her from the sun. "I'll be back in half a mo'," he told her. "Roast beef all right for you?"

She nodded her thanks, and watched him hurry off toward the side door of the pub. While he was gone, she thought about the news Howard Clark had given her. George Lewis must have had a compelling reason to risk embezzling money. He must have known it would come to light eventually. If she knew the reason, she might be closer to finding out what really happened the night the house caught fire.

Perhaps Mr. Lewis's brother could help her. It was odd that he and his wife didn't take Emma in. What kind of brother was he to allow that helpless child to be taken to an orphanage?

She would visit him that very afternoon, before she returned to Crickling Green. She wanted to meet the man who could so easily turn his back on his brother's child.

Not only that, he might be able to shed light on George

Lewis's financial situation. There could have been many
reasons why he would have needed money so desperately.
She frowned, trying to imagine the kind of circumstances
that would compel an apparently respected, honorable man
to steal.

Reggie interrupted her thoughts, returning with hefty
roast beef sandwiches, her glass of cider, and a foaming
glass of ale. Sitting opposite her, he gave her a rueful grin.

"Can't hear yourself think in there," he said, nodding at
the pub, where echoes of the uproar inside floated across
the grass. "Good job you decided to sit out here."

"It's very pleasant out here." Meredith helped herself to
a sandwich, wondering what Sylvia Montrose would say if
she saw the sedate headmistress of Bellehaven sharing
lunch in a beer garden with the handyman.

For some reason a vision of Stuart Hamilton popped
into her mind, and for a brief instant she wondered what he
would think of her rather indelicate behavior. Not that it
mattered to her, she hastily told herself, and concentrated
instead on what Reggie was saying.

". . . so I gave him a drink and a slap on his rump."

Meredith raised her eyebrows. "I beg your pardon?"

Reggie looked confused. "Major. I was saying as how I
felt sorry for him, so I gave him a drink of water."

"Oh, I see." Meredith took another bite of the sandwich.

"He does good for an old horse."

"Yes, he does." She reached for her cider and took a sip.
It warmed her with a pleasant sensation as it went down.

"Course, it must be hard on him, all this unaccustomed
exercise."

Something in Reggie's tone alerted her, and she peered
at him. "Are you worried about Major?"

Reggie had just bitten a chunk out of his sandwich, and
he chewed on it with fierce determination until he could
swallow. "Well, m'm, to tell the truth, I was wondering
how he would hold up if you intended to do much more
running around like this."

He must have seen her expression change, since he added quickly, "Not that I'm not enjoying it, m'm. It's right nice to be out and about instead of cooped up in the school all the time. Not that I mind that, of course. I mean, I like my job and all, but it makes a change, dunnit, to get out now and again, and . . ."

His voice trailed off as she continued to look at him.

"It's none of my business, m'm. Forget I said anything."

Feeling sorry for him, she put down her sandwich with a sigh. "Reggie, I know you're concerned about Major, and I don't blame you. I've been thinking about him myself. I've considered asking Mr. Hamilton if we may acquire another horse, so that Major has a chance to rest now and then."

Reggie's face filled with hope. "Does that mean you'll be doing some more running around then, Mrs. L?"

Meredith paused to consider whether or not she objected to being reduced to an initial, then dismissed the matter as trivial. There was something far more important to be addressed, and she needed to take care of it right then and there.

It was becoming increasingly apparent that she could not keep her investigating venture a secret from Reggie for long. What's more, knowing her handyman's lively curiosity, in attempting to find out exactly what she was up to, he could very well expose her activities to the wrong person.

Deliberately she erased the vision of Stuart Hamilton. The only safe avenue open to her was to take Reggie into her confidence. As much as he needed to know, anyway. She could only hope that she could trust in his discretion.

Realizing that he was still waiting for her answer, she took another sip of cider. "Reggie, I need to tell you something, but before I do, I must ask for your sworn oath that it will go no further. I must insist on complete and utter secrecy, no matter who may ask you questions. Do I have your word?"

Reggie's dark blue eyes gleamed with excitement. Laying

a hand on his heart, he declared in a solemn voice, "I swear on my dear departed mother's grave that no secrets you tell me shall ever pass me lips. Not to another living soul. So help me."

Satisfied, she gave him a brief nod. "I'm taking you into my confidence, Reggie, because there may be a time when I need you by my side. But if word of any of this gets out, it could be the end of employment at Bellehaven for both of us."

Practically jumping up and down with anticipation, Reggie leaned forward. "Is it illegal, then? You're breaking the law?"

"Oh, good heavens, I hope not."

"Like when you went inside that burnt house?"

She stared at him. "That was illegal?"

He shrugged. "Well, I don't know for sure, of course, but it could be."

Horrified, she quickly swallowed a mouthful of cider, then choked on it when it stung her throat. "But the house wasn't locked or anything," she said hoarsely when she could speak.

Reggie looked doubtful. "Well, it could be all right, then, I suppose, but—"

"Well, never mind that now." Meredith hunted in her handbag for her handkerchief, found it, and delicately dabbed her mouth. If she had broken the law, it was too late to worry about it now. Tucking the handkerchief back in her handbag, she said more calmly, "The point is, I'm conducting an investigation into the deaths of the Lewis family."

The shock on Reggie's face was comical. "You're working for the bobbies?"

"No, no!" She held on to her glass for comfort. "This is entirely on my own, for my own reasons."

Reggie frowned. "Who's the Lewis family?"

"The people who died in that house fire."

His face cleared. "Oh, them." He thought about it, then frowned again. "You knew them?"

"Not exactly." She paused, then decided it wasn't completely a lie, though she did seem to be bending the truth a lot lately. She added, "I am well acquainted with a member of the family, however."

"Oh, all right then." His frown returned. "Why did they ask you to investigate? Why didn't they go to the bobbies?"

"Because the . . . ah . . . constables don't believe it wasn't an accident."

"It wasn't?" Reggie eyes widened. "How'd you know that?"

"I don't, for certain." She met his gaze steadily. "That's what I'm investigating."

"Ah, I see." He sat back. "I think. So that's why you're doing all this running around."

"Yes. I have people I need to talk to about the family. Which brings me to the subject in hand. Are you familiar with an ironmongers named Spicers?"

"Spicers? Yeah, I've seen it in the High Street in Witcheston."

"Yes, well, apparently other members of the family live in a flat over the shop. I'd like to go and talk to them before we return to Bellehaven."

Reggie looked worried. He pulled a pocket watch from the back pocket of his trousers and peered at it. "It's getting late, Mrs. L. Don't you have to be back at the school to take classes?"

"Not this afternoon. I gave the students an assignment to do in their rooms instead. Just in case I was delayed in returning to the school."

He nodded, and put the watch back in his pocket. "I have just one question, m'm, if you don't mind."

She smiled at him. "Fire away, Reggie. I'll answer if I can."

"Is this investigation of yours likely to be dangerous? I mean, should I be carrying a pistol or something, in case we get into trouble?"

She almost laughed. "Reggie, I assure you, we won't be in any more danger than losing a handrail. I promise you won't need a pistol to defend me."

He looked vastly relieved. "Well, then, I'm your man.
Just tell me what you want me to do and I'll be there."

"Right now all I want you to do is drive me to the ironmongers. That's if you think Major is up to it?"

"What?" He shook his head. "Oh, yes, m'm. He'll be
fine. He's had a rest, though I think he'll be happy once he
gets back to his stable again."

"Yes, I really must tackle Mr. Hamilton about another
horse." She finished the last of her sandwich, then drained
her glass. The cider had warmed her tummy and relaxed
her, giving her the comfortable feeling that she was capable of tackling anything that came her way.

True, her head felt a little light when she stood up, and
her step was a trifle unsteady as she followed Reggie around
to the courtyard, but altogether she felt quite pleased with
herself, and the way she was handling this adventure.

To be quite honest with herself, she found it all most
exhilarating. She couldn't wait to meet George Lewis's
brother and find out why he might have been driven to
steal a great deal of money, and risk everything worth
having in his life.

The High Street seemed even more crowded as Major
drew them past the shops that lined the pavement. Meredith
would have loved to gaze at all the fascinating goods in the
windows of the haberdashery and the costumer's, and especially the intriguing display in the art shop window.

Time was of the essence, however, since to be absent
from the school too long would be bound to arouse the notice of Sylvia Montrose, who would duly report it to Stuart
Hamilton.

As it was, Meredith thought with a stab of guilt, she was
taking far too long and enjoying this day out far too much.
Since she was already in town, however, it would be foolish
to pass up this chance to question George Lewis's brother.

At last Reggie brought Major to a halt at the very end of
the High Street, and Meredith clambered out of the coach,
eager to get the meeting over with and return to Bellehaven.

The woman who answered her knock on the door looked as if she had just been aroused from a deep slumber. Her hair was in disarray, the floral frock she wore seemed to have been thrown on in haste, and her expression was none too welcoming.

Meredith began to wonder if perhaps she'd made a mistake in insisting Reggie stay behind with the carriage to wait for her. Quickly she introduced herself. "I'm so sorry to intrude," she added when the woman just stood there with a blank and rather hostile look on her face. "I wonder if I might speak with your husband. I believe he's the brother of a late acquaintance of mine, Mr. George Lewis."

At the mention of the name, the woman's face changed. "You're a friend of George's?" She glanced over her shoulder, hesitated, then with obvious reluctance beckoned at Meredith to enter.

"I'm afraid it's a mess," she said, rather unnecessarily, as Meredith picked her way over discarded newspapers, a bag of knitting, a pair of work boots, and a dish of what appeared to be the remains of a cat's dinner.

She was right about the cat, as one jumped off the settee with a yowl as she approached.

"I wasn't expecting visitors." The woman sat down on a rocking chair that emitted a loud groan as she leaned back. "I'm Amanda, Claude's wife. He's at work right now, won't be back until six."

Meredith looked at her in dismay. "Oh, I was rather hoping to meet him."

Amanda Lewis gave her a look of pure speculation. "Did George's lawyer send you here?"

She wasn't expecting the question and floundered for a moment. "Er . . . not exactly . . . no . . . that is . . ."

Amanda's face registered acute disappointment. "Oh, I was hoping George had left something for us in his will. I thought maybe he'd had a change of heart."

Meredith frowned. "I beg your pardon?"

"I thought he'd changed his mind about the money

Claude wanted." Amanda paused. "Would you like a cup of tea?"

Glancing at the cat hairs and dust covering every surface in the room, Meredith inwardly shuddered. "Thank you, no. I have just finished a meal. I do appreciate the offer, though."

Amanda nodded. "I'd better warn you, Claude won't want to talk about George. He's never forgiven him for refusing to lend him the money when the business went bad."

"The business?"

The cat squeezed out from under Amanda's chair and leapt onto her lap. She stroked it for a moment before answering. "Claude was doing all right with the shop. Right in the middle of the High Street it was, with customers passing by every day. Couldn't have had a better spot." She sighed as the cat settled down on her lap. "We had a nice house with a lovely garden where the children had room to run around and play. Servants to look after us, and everything."

"You have children?" Meredith looked around the room for a photograph.

"Two boys and a girl. They're at school right now." Amanda glanced at the clock on the mantelpiece. "They should be home soon."

Glancing around the room again, Meredith wondered how a family of five survived together in such cramped surroundings. "What happened to your house?" Realizing that was an impolite question, she quickly added, "If you don't mind me asking."

Amanda shrugged. "It's no secret. Claude sold farming equipment, and he was doing well. Then someone bought a lot of expensive equipment from him and never paid him. Claude took him to court, but the farmer had a really sharp lawyer. They said the equipment was no good, that it wasn't worth half of what the farmer paid for it."

"I'm so sorry. That must have been a terrible hardship."

"It was." Amanda stared down at the cat purring on her lap. "Claude didn't have the money to pay for the lease. He asked George to lend him what he needed. He said George could easily have lent it to him, he had plenty to spare, but he told Claude he didn't trust his business practices. Said Claude would lose everything and wouldn't be able to pay him back."

"How awful, not to trust your own brother."

"Well, they weren't real brothers, you see. George's father took Claude in off the street when he was five. Never knew his real name so Mr. Lewis gave him his name, though he never did make it legal."

"Still, if he was treated like a brother . . ."

Amanda's mouth twisted in a wry smile. "George was a banker, wasn't he. He knew all about how to handle money. Besides, he was probably right about Claude. My husband was always giving stuff away. Said it made him feel important. He wanted people to think he had plenty of money to throw around, when really we were barely scraping by because of what he spent on the house and gardens. It was all for show." She uttered a bitter laugh. "Lot of good it does him now."

Meredith leaned forward. "That must have been really difficult for you."

"I always knew it wouldn't last, and I was right. We lost the shop, couldn't pay the servants what we owed them, so we had to sell the house to pay our bills." The despair in her eyes when she looked around the room gave Meredith chills. "This is all we can afford for now. It costs a lot to clothe and feed a family. I take in laundry, but it's hard work and doesn't pay much."

"I'm so sorry." Meredith was feeling more depressed by the minute. "I can understand why your husband felt such bitterness toward Mr. Lewis."

"He'll never get over it." Amanda picked up the cat and buried her face in its fur for a moment. "He blamed George for all our troubles. Don't tell him I told you, but he took up drinking after we lost the house. Goes out every night to the Pig and Whistle, he does, and sometimes he doesn't come home all night."

"I'm sorry. Something like that can be very difficult to live with."

"Yes it is." The cat yowled and she put it back down on her lap. "The funny thing is, I don't think George had the money to lend to Claude. They say he embezzled money from the bank, though I don't believe that for one minute. George wouldn't do something like that."

Surprised to hear her defend her brother-in-law after he'd caused them so much trouble, Meredith asked, "Why is that?"

Amanda gave her a sharp look. "Well, you knew George, didn't you? He was a good man, not weak, like my Claude. He turned down a life of luxury to stay with his wife."

The cat yowled again, and she picked it up and lowered it to the floor. "There's this really rich widow, Blanche Pettigrew, she owns the Sandalwood Estate out on the east highway. She wanted George, from what I hear, and was at the bank every day offering him anything he wanted if he'd leave his wife and go away with her. He could have lived like a king, but he chose to stay with Dorothy and the children. That's the kind of man he was, but then you probably know that."

"Yes, of course." Feeling guilty for her deception, Meredith shifted uneasily on her chair.

"He wouldn't have been happy, anyway." Amanda brushed cat hairs from her lap. "From what Dorothy told me, that Pettigrew woman was really demanding. Then there was her nephew . . ." Amanda paused, frowning in concentration. "Will Barnard, that's his name. He lives with Mrs. Pettigrew. She doesn't have any children of her own. Will was really nasty to George. Probably thought he would steal his inheritance. He would have given George plenty of grief, I'm sure of that."

"It certainly sounds like it."

Amanda nodded. "Well, like I said, Claude won't want to talk about George. To tell you the truth, Mrs. Llewellyn, it's best that you don't wait for him. Like I said, he goes drinking after work, and not just beer, neither. If he comes home with a bellyful of spirits and you start talking about George . . . well, it might not be good for you, that's all I'm saying."

"Of course. I quite understand." Meredith rose to her feet.

"Then again, he might not come home at all." Sighing, Amanda pushed herself out of her chair. "It's getting more and more frequent. He was out all night the night George and Dorothy died. Said he passed out on the way home and didn't wake up until the next morning." Her face suddenly crumpled. "That poor little baby. My heart breaks for that child. And Emma . . . such a sweet child. To die all alone like that. I would have taken her, but Claude put his foot down. Said we couldn't afford to take her in."

Meredith tried to remind herself that Emma would probably have died even if she had been taken in by Amanda. But at least she would have passed on with familiar faces around her, instead of strangers in that dreadful place.

Deciding that she didn't like Claude Lewis one tiny bit, Meredith moved toward the door. It was just as well he hadn't been home, she thought, as she descended the dark and grimy stairs to the street. She might have given him a piece of her mind. After what she had heard about him, that would most likely have been quite an unpleasant experience.

Claude Lewis sounded like the kind of man one would go out of his way to avoid. Hostile and bitter—not the sort of man one would want to offend.

She paused at the bottom of the steps, one hand on the door leading to the street. Hostile enough to burn the house down? Amanda had told her that Claude had stayed out that whole night. He would know how to get into the house. He could have easily attacked his brother in his sleep, perhaps his wife, too, and set fire to the house in a drunken rage.

Definitely a possibility. But how on earth would she prove it? Frustrated, she stepped out onto the street. This detective business was far more complicated than she'd ever imagined. Perhaps she should just go to the police with her suspicions and let them find out what really happened that night.

It was definitely something she needed to think about.

Chapter 10

"Reggie, I need to stop by the Pig and Whistle again on our way home."

Opening the door of the carriage, Reggie looked at Meredith in surprise. "You want to go back to the pub, m'm? But it's closed for the afternoon. Won't be open now until five o'clock."

"I don't want a drink, Reggie." Meredith climbed up onto her seat. "I want to speak to the proprietor. I'm sure you can arrange that."

"Well, yes, m'm, but—" His expression changed from puzzlement to apprehension. "Ah . . . I see. You want to investigate him."

"Not exactly."

"Someone else at the pub then?"

Meredith leaned forward and lowered her voice. "You and I will get along much better, Reggie, if you'll stop asking so many questions. Be assured I will tell you anything you need to know. In fact, I would like you to accompany me when I question the proprietor."

"Oh, of course, m'm." Looking excited at the prospect, Reggie closed the door and climbed up onto his perch.

As they jogged once more down the High Street, Meredith went over the conversation she'd had with Amanda. It certainly seemed that her husband had strong reasons for hating his brother. It was hard to imagine anyone's hatred being powerful enough to kill an entire family. It was terrible, indeed, what too much spirits could do to the mind.

Deep in thought, she was startled when Reggie brought the carriage to a halt. They had arrived at the Pig and Whistle without her noticing.

The proprietor, a rotund gentleman with a nose that glowed like the evening sun, seemed most unsettled when Reggie presented her. Although he seemed reluctant to talk to her, he graciously invited her and Reggie into his parlor, and offered her a glass of ale.

"Thank you, Mr. Willoughby, but I have already partaken of your excellent brew and quite enjoyed it." Seated on a sagging armchair, Meredith smiled up at him. "I really think it would be wise to refrain from enjoying another."

Reggie, on the other hand, leapt at the chance of free ale. He sat across the room, frothing glass in hand, while Mr. Willoughby took a seat on the other side of the fireplace.

"My wife will be sorry to have missed your visit, Mrs. Llewellyn," he said as he settled himself more comfortably. "She's visiting relatives in Brighton at the moment."

Meredith nodded. "It's a very pleasant town to visit."

"It is, indeed." He gave her a hard stare. "Now what, may I ask, is the purpose of your visit today?"

"I have some questions about one of your customers, a Mr. Claude Lewis. I was hoping you'd be able to answer them for me."

Watching his face closely, she saw wariness in his eyes. "What's old Claude been up to now?"

"Ah, so you do know him."

"Yes, indeed. He's a regular at the Pig and Whistle."

"Yes, so I understand." She paused, arranging the words in her head. "I expect you know he recently lost his brother and family."

Willoughby shook his head. He had a long, wispy mustache and muttonchops, and looked rather like an aging walrus. "Such a terrible tragedy, that. Poor little mite, the daughter, watching her whole family go up in flames, then getting sick and dying like that. Terrible. Terrible."

"It was, indeed." Meredith drew a steadying breath. "I don't suppose you happen to remember that night?"

"As a matter of fact, I do." Willoughby rubbed his chin with a roughened hand. "It was pouring with rain that night. Good job it was, it helped to put out the fire or that whole house would have burned to the ground. Not that it helped the Lewises much, of course. I heard the fire wagon go by. They had to pass right by here on the way out of town."

"So you remember the night well."

Willoughby nodded. "Funny thing, I spoke to Claude right after we heard the fire bell ringing. Sounds like someone's got a good one burning, I sez to Claude. He agreed with me, never dreaming it was his own family going up in smoke."

Meredith suppressed a shiver. "So he was here all that evening?"

"All evening and all night long." His expression changed. "Did his wife send you?"

Meredith frowned. "No, she didn't. She doesn't know I'm here."

Willoughby puffed out his breath. "Oh, good. I thought maybe she was checking up on him, so to speak."

"I think she knows where her husband spends his evenings," Meredith said primly.

"Ah, but she don't know with whom, do she." Willoughby glanced at Reggie, who leaned forward, hanging on to every word. "Perhaps I shouldn't say."

"Shouldn't say what, Mr. Willoughby?" Meredith sent Reggie a warning look to keep silent.

"Well, let us just say that Claude wasn't exactly alone that night, if you get my meaning. Getting to be quite a habit with him, it is."

"I see." Meredith gathered up her handbag and stood. Willoughby stood up with her, while Reggie rose more slowly, draining his glass as he did so. "I think you've answered my questions satisfactorily, Mr. Willoughby. I'll be on my way now." She glared at Reggie, whose head was tilted back in an effort to drain every drop of ale.

Willoughby rubbed his hands together, as if he felt a chill. "I'd be obliged if you didn't bring my name into this," he said as he led her to the door. "I don't want Claude taking his temper out on me when his wife finds out what he's been up to and all."

"You misunderstand me, Mr. Willoughby." Meredith paused in the doorway. "Mrs. Lewis will not find out from me or from my driver that her husband is not to be trusted. I'll leave that in the hands of the gossips. I'm sure word will get to her sooner or later. Thank you for your time."

She swept out of the building and hurried over to the carriage. Claude Lewis may not be a murderer, as she had at first suspected, but he was every bit as despicable as she had imagined. She felt quite sorry for Amanda. She deserved better. Much better.

As for her investigation, all her efforts had revealed nothing, except that Claude was obviously not guilty of setting fire to his brother's house. What's more, she was at a complete loss as to how to proceed from there.

Walking into the school later that afternoon, Meredith was surprised to see Felicity hurrying toward her. She had warned both of her friends to keep her absence a secret from Sylvia Montrose, if at all possible. Judging by the expression on Felicity's face, it seemed likely that one of them had failed to do so.

To her utter dismay, it was worse than that.

"Hamilton," Felicity barked as soon as she was within earshot. "He's waiting for you in your office and he's not too happy."

"Drat." Meredith glanced at the grandfather clock in the hall. Almost half past three. "How long has he been here?"

"Since noon. He had dinner in the dining room with the rest of us. Sat there with a face like thunder."

"What did you tell him?"

"Only that you had important errands to run." Felicity shook her head. "If you are going to insist on running all over town to assist someone who has already passed on, you might want to consider that what goes on in the hereafter is not nearly as important as your life in the here and now."

Already feeling out of sorts after her fruitless outing, which had been little more than a waste of time, not to mention the looming task of placating an angry Hamilton, Meredith sharpened her tongue. "I'm well aware of that, Felicity. You can stop worrying, however. Since it appears I am not capable of unraveling the mystery surrounding the deaths of the Lewis family, I am simply . . ." She flung out a hand in a dramatic gesture. "Giving up."

Felicity stared at her in astonishment. "Giving up? *You?* I don't believe it."

"Well, believe it." Meredith lifted her hands to unpin her hat. "My head is spinning with all the perhaps and maybes, the ifs and buts. I'm quite done with it all." Hat in hand, she marched down the corridor to her office, turned the handle, and thrust the door open.

Hamilton stood at the window, his back toward her as he gazed out at the lawns. Roger Platt sat at her desk, laboriously writing in a ledger. He looked up as she stepped inside the room and closed the door behind her.

"Oh, there you are, Mrs. Llewellyn," he murmured in his smarmy voice. "We were wondering what had become of you." He glanced at the broad back of Hamilton, as if expecting him to turn and vent his wrath on his wayward headmistress.

Instead, the gentleman kept his gaze on the view outside. "Mr. Pratt," he said, his voice devoid of emotion, "I would appreciate it if you would leave the room. I have matters to discuss with Mrs. Llewellyn."

Meredith's stomach gave a nervous little jump.

"It's Platt, sir." Roger sent her a look that could only be described as patronizing. He closed the ledger, stuck it under his arm, and left the room.

Meredith hung her hat on the hat stand, then moved around the desk to her chair and sat down. Being in the familiar position gave her confidence, and she directed her gaze on Hamilton's back. "Good afternoon, Mr. Hamilton."

"Mrs. Llewellyn." He turned then, and again her stomach skipped when she saw his stern expression. "I must ask you to explain your lengthy absence today. I understand you made use of the horse and carriage."

She met his gaze, even though the fluttering in her stomach was becoming quite uncomfortable. "Yes, I did. I needed to go into Witcheston to run some errands."

"I see." He pursed his lips, and her insides reacted in that ridiculous predictable manner. "I hope it had nothing to do with your health?"

She gave him a blank look. "My health?"

"Yes, I . . . ah . . . everyone I talked to went to great lengths to avoid telling me the reason for your absence, so I . . . ah . . . was wondering if perhaps you were visiting a physician."

Good heavens. Could the man possibly be concerned about her? Smiling, she answered, "I was not visiting a doctor, Mr. Hamilton. I am in good health. My visit to Witcheston concerned another matter which had to be attended to today. My absence in no way affected the students, since I gave them an assignment in lieu of their class."

He continued to stare at her, as if expecting her to explain further. She glanced down at her hands, unwilling to lie to him, and unable to tell him the truth.

"Well," he said at last. "I'm happy to hear you are not ailing. I do hope your . . . matter was resolved to your satisfaction."

"Thank you, it was." *Not really*, she added inwardly, but it would hardly be prudent to inform him that she was investigating the possibility of murder and had failed miserably in her attempts.

"I called today to ask how Pratt was working out."

She studied him briefly, wondering if he deliberately mispronounced the young man's name, and if it was some kind of test. Deciding she was being foolish, she murmured, "Mr. *Platt* seems adequate so far. He hasn't been here long enough to give a fair evaluation of his skills."

"Quite, quite." His gaze sharpened. "No . . . ah . . . problems with the young ladies, then, as you feared?"

Remembering the incident in the music room, Meredith bit her tongue. "Nothing that I wasn't able to contend with," she said evenly.

Hamilton nodded. "Good, good." He hesitated for a moment, then added, "Then I'll be off and leave you to get on with your work."

He started to move away, and deciding this was as good a time as any, Meredith held up her hand. "One moment, Mr. Hamilton, if I may, I'd like to have a word with you about something?"

"Of course."

He looked expectant, and Meredith glanced down at her hands again. If he was waiting for her to tell him where she had gone that morning, he was doomed to disappointment. She paused for a moment, then lifted her head.

"I was wondering if it is at all possible for us to acquire another horse."

His eyebrows shot up almost to his hairline. "Another *horse*? Whatever for?"

Taking offense at his tone, Meredith bristled. "To pull the carriage, of course. Major is getting old and I don't like to burden him. He tires easily, and could do an injury to himself if pushed too far."

Hamilton's eyebrows lowered only slightly. "I wasn't aware that you used the carriage that much."

She took a deep breath. This investigation was causing far more complications than she had ever imagined. It was definitely time to reconsider her course of action. "I'm finding the need to go farther afield in the interests of the school," she said, hoping it wasn't too much of a lie.

After all, she consoled herself, being badgered by a ghost desperate for her help affected her concentration, which adversely affected her performance in the classroom. Therefore, she was quite justified in trying to remedy the situation in the only way she knew how—to clear the way for the ghost to pass on.

Hamilton's skepticism was evident by his expression. "I trust this is not a permanent condition. If so, I shall have to assign such duties to Pratt. We can't have our headmistress obliged to run all over the countryside while her pupils are confined to their rooms with assignments."

Meredith was beginning to wish heartily that she'd never mentioned acquiring another horse. After all, if she no longer intended to pursue the matter of the Lewis family's deaths, there would be no need for another horse.

"I can see that my request is not favorably received," she said, trying to keep the resentment out of her voice. "Therefore, I withdraw it. We will make do with Major."

He continued to regard her until she was forced to drop her gaze. "Very well. I wish you good day."

She didn't look up again until the door had closed behind him. Insufferable man! Why did he make her feel as though she were a child in the presence of a forbidding parent? What did he know about managing a school, anyway? Why couldn't he simply trust her judgment instead of questioning her every move?

Thoroughly incensed, she glared as the door opened and Roger Platt strolled in.

He took one look at her expression and his grin faded. "Mr. Hamilton said I should return, but if you wish me to leave you alone—"

"No. I have a rehearsal in the music room in ten minutes." She got up from her chair. "You may have my desk back."

"Yes, m'm." He waited for her to move out from the desk, then laid the ledger down. "I trust Mr. Hamilton had no problems with my work?"

Obviously he was concerned she might have complained

about him, and rightly so, Meredith thought, with unaccustomed malice. "Not so far, as yet," she said, her voice curt. "You may carry on, Mr. Platt. I need you to start work on those proposals for the next fund-raiser."

"Yes, m'm." He sounded subdued, and she allowed herself a little smile of satisfaction. That young gentleman needed a firm hand, and she was quite capable of administering it, as he would no doubt find out if he crossed her again.

Frowning, she charged down the corridor to the music room, hoping that her choir were on their best behavior so that she could restore her good humor.

Meredith retired early to bed that night, exhausted from the tumult of the day. The rehearsal had not gone well. The students had begun to show signs of stage fright, with only one more rehearsal before their big day.

After several false starts they finally got through the program, but it still sounded ragged, and Meredith had to seriously consider adding another rehearsal.

Moreover, both Felicity and Essie wanted to know every detail of her visit to Witcheston. Depressed by her lack of progress, Meredith was in no mood to discuss it, and it didn't help when Felicity chided her for giving up so easily.

What with trying to keep up with her duties at the school, keep Roger Platt in his place, and avoid arousing Stuart Hamilton's curiosity about her activities, Meredith just could not envision wasting any more time on such a fruitless endeavor.

Still trying to make up her mind whether or not she should go to the constabulary with her suspicions, she fell into an uneasy slumber, only to be awakened shortly after by the familiar chill in the room.

"Emma?" She sat up in bed, squinting in the darkness at the green glow in the corner. It seemed to fade, then burn a little brighter. Reaching for her lamp, she sighed.

Somehow she would have to make the child understand that she was unable to help her. She wasn't even certain that a murder had been committed, much less who could have been responsible and why.

The light flared from her match, and then, as she held it to the wick, the warm glow filled the room. She couldn't see Emma clearly, just a vague shape of her enveloped in a wispy cloud that ebbed and flowed.

"I went to your house," Meredith said, peering hard at the cloud in the hopes of seeing Emma's face. "I saw your room. It was very nice."

The mist thickened, then faded again.

Meredith tried again. "I found the horse statuette. It was on the floor of your parents' bedroom."

This time the cloud grew bigger, swirling around as if a tornado were whirling inside it. The vague figure in the middle became more distinct—the outline of a child, then her face, then her features.

At last, Meredith could see her expression. The child was crying.

"I believe someone else was there," Meredith said quickly. "Someone who wanted to hurt your parents. But I don't know how to find out who it was, or even to prove that the fire wasn't an accident. I tried, but—"

She broke off as Emma raised an arm. The child's finger pointed to her bedside table.

Following the gesture, Meredith frowned. There was nothing on the table but the oil lamp, its flame wafting back and forth as if caught in a draft.

She looked back at Emma, whose finger still steadily pointed at the table. "I don't understand, Emma. What are you trying to tell me?"

Emma's fingers closed into a fist, and slowly, she lifted her elbow and tilted her hand inward.

Meredith frowned. "What are you doing, child?"

Once more Emma's finger pointed, only this time she jabbed it at the table, then raised her thin elbow again and tilted her hand.

Striving to understand, Meredith leaned forward. "Are you pouring something?"

The ghostly hand fell to the child's side.

Shaking her head in bewilderment, Meredith looked at the table again. It had to have something to do with the lamp. She envisioned Emma holding it, then tilting it . . .

"Oh, my goodness!" She stared across the room at Emma's ghost. "Someone poured the oil from the lamp onto your parents' bed and set fire to it." She reached for the lamp and held it up. "Is that what you're trying to tell me?"

Immediately the child's image began to fade.

Meredith cried out. "No, wait! You have to tell me who did this! Give me some sort of sign . . ." Her voice trailed off. She was talking to empty space. Emma and the cloud that surrounded her had disappeared.

Meredith set the lamp back onto the table. She was no longer tired. Moreover, now she felt compelled to continue the hunt. That child had actually seen someone kill her parents and set fire to their bed. Eventually Emma would find a way to tell her the identity of that person. She was sure of it.

As long as Emma kept giving her signs, she would keep on trying to find out who had killed her family and caused her to lose her own life. The child must be avenged, and somehow, Meredith was determined to see that it happened.

Chapter 11

"It's all your fault." Olivia sat back on her heels and brushed a strand of dark hair from her eyes, leaving a trail of dust across her forehead. "It will take us weeks to clean out this filthy place."

Grace stared at her. "Why is it my fault? Weren't you the one who said no one would know we'd be gone?"

"No one would've known if you hadn't told Wilky where we were going." Olivia flung out a grubby hand. "Now look at us. We have to spend our afternoon off every week cleaning out this awful, dirty attic until Mona's satisfied with it, and you know she'll hang it out as long as possible. She was frothing at the mouth when she told us."

Grace pulled a tennis racket and press from a pile of clutter in the corner. "It won't take us long if we work really hard."

Olivia picked up an armful of curtains and threw them into a box. Dust danced in the ray of sunlight cast through the tiny window above her head. "Look at that. All that dust is going into our lungs and choking us."

She started to cough, and Grace shook her head. "If you're going to moan about it all afternoon, I'm not going to listen. So there." She took a wide swipe through the air with the tennis racket. The press on the end weighed it down and it caught the edge of a box, tilting it over and spilling the contents across the floor.

"Now look what you've done!" Olivia's scowl contorted her face. "You can pick that lot up by yourself."

Putting down the tennis racket, Grace squatted beside her. "Look at all these old photographs!" She picked one up and peered at it, holding it up to the light to see it more clearly. "This must be the people who lived here before Bellehaven was a school. Look at their old-fashioned clothes."

"Where? Let me see." Olivia took the picture from her. "They look like right toffs, don't they. Though the young one's handsome enough."

Grace snatched the picture back. "He reminds me of Mrs. Llewellyn's new assistant with that dark hair and eyes." She started picking up the rest of the photographs, looking at each one. "I passed him in the hallway this morning."

Olivia shrugged and turned back to her task. "He's all right, I suppose. A bit toffee-nosed."

"I think he's handsome." Grace held the pictures to her chest. "I wouldn't mind going for a walk with him in the dark."

Olivia snorted. "Go on with you. Men like Mr. Platt don't go walking anywhere with the likes of us."

Feeling a jab of resentment, Grace jutted out her bottom lip. "So who says? I bet I could get him to ask me out, so there."

Olivia sat back and stared at her. "What's got into you, Grace Parker? You don't even like boys, or so you're always telling me."

Grace started putting the pictures back in the box. "I don't like those common louts in the village, like the ones you're always talking to outside the pub." She looked at the first picture she'd picked up. "I could go for someone like him, though. Someone like Mr. Platt."

"Yeah, well, Mr. Platt ain't going to oblige, not with you

being below his station and all, so you might as well stop the daydreaming." Olivia tugged at a box that was half buried under a pile of eiderdowns. "I wonder what's in here."

Reluctantly, Grace put the picture back with the others. Olivia was probably right, but it wasn't going to stop her dreaming. One day she was going to have a fine house and servants. It was the dream that kept her going when things got her down. Like today.

Olivia's gasp interrupted her thoughts. "Blimey, Grace. Look at this." She scrambled to her feet, holding the exquisite frock up against her body. "It looks like a wedding gown."

Grace touched the fine lace with reverent fingers. "Oh, my, look at that. It's beautiful."

"Do you think it'd fit me?" Olivia twirled around so that the skirt gently folded around her ankles. "I think I'll keep this for when I get married."

Grace scrambled to her feet. "You can't! It'd be stealing."

"Stealing from who?" Olivia held the dress away from her to study it. "It don't belong to no one now, or they wouldn't have left it here all crumpled up in a box."

"What if it belongs to one of the teachers?" Grace gasped. "Or Miss Fingle?"

Olivia let out a shout of laughter. "Can you see that old crony wearing something like this? Not on your life. No, no one knows it's here so no one will know I took it." She folded the gown over her arm and glared at her friend. "And don't you dare go telling no one I got it or I'll never ever be your friend again."

Grace shook her head. "I won't tell no one, Olivia, I swear it. But it's bad luck for you to take it, I just know it. It will mean nothing but bad things happening to you."

"Don't be daft." Olivia reached for the box and carefully packed the gown back into it. "Look, there's a veil, and gloves and everything. I'll wear it all the day I get married."

Grace knew it was no use arguing with her friend. Still, she had a nasty feeling in the pit of her stomach. She didn't understand why she thought the gown would bring bad luck, she just knew it would. All she could hope for was that some of it didn't rub off on her.

Much to Meredith's surprise and gratification, Reggie seemed able to find his way to Blanche Pettigrew's estate without too much trouble. She was beginning to change her opinion of the young man. Although she abhorred his somewhat reckless attitude and occasional impertinence, she had to admit that her handyman could be quite enterprising at times.

Having told herself that Hamilton was unlikely to return to Bellehaven anytime soon, she had taken advantage of a free morning to visit the Sandalwood Estate.

She had woken up that morning with a renewed determination to solve the puzzle of the Lewis family's deaths. She no longer had any doubt that someone had deliberately set the fire. Emma's ghost had convinced her of that.

If she could find out why George Lewis had embezzled funds, she might be closer to finding the killer. She wasn't sure why she thought Blanche Pettigrew could help her, except for Amanda Lewis saying that Mrs. Pettigrew's nephew was apparently hostile toward George.

It had crossed her mind that perhaps George might have had an assignation with Mrs. Pettigrew, and was paying the nephew to keep quiet about it. Though if the young man was living with a rich aunt, presumably he'd be in no need of funds.

Conjecture. Pure conjecture, which was all she seemed capable of doing. It was quite frustrating.

The Sandalwood Estate stood high on a hill, which afforded a remarkable view of the downs and Witcheston in the distance. Standing on the steps leading up to the wide front porch, Meredith gazed down at the town. The streets looked like a miniature maze, lined with little toy houses.

A white church spire poked up against the sky, gleaming in the morning sun, and beyond it spread a carpet of dark green forest that gradually faded into the mist.

So intrigued with the view was she, that a voice spoke before she realized the door had opened in answer to her summons. Turning, she confronted a haughty-looking gentleman dressed in a butler's uniform. Wings of gray marked his dark hair above his ears, and his gray eyes regarded her with mild disdain.

Hastily she introduced herself, saying she wished to see Mrs. Pettigrew on a private matter.

The butler ushered her into the hallway, then disappeared down a long corridor, the walls of which were covered with ancestors' portraits.

While she waited, Meredith studied the Victorian hallstand—a magnificent piece with ornate carvings of a lion's head surrounding the gilded framed mirror.

The butler's voice spoke behind her, startling her. "Madam will see you now, if you will kindly follow me."

As her feet sank into the dark blue and cream carpet, Meredith could understand why she hadn't heard the butler's footsteps. It was like walking on pillows.

The butler paused in front of a set of double doors and tapped lightly on one polished panel. A thin voice answered from inside, and he turned the handles of both doors and pushed them open.

"Mrs. Llewellyn, madam," he announced, then stood aside to allow Meredith to enter.

The woman who stood to greet her was amazingly beautiful. Though no longer young, her figure was that of a young girl's, tightly laced into a pale lilac tea gown made of extraordinary fine cotton and lace.

A quick glance around the room left no doubt of the widow's exquisite taste and certainly the wherewithal to indulge it. The purple sateen curtains at the windows were of the finest quality, and the beautiful mahogany sideboard with the satinwood inlaid surface was undoubtedly Sheraton.

The fireplace dominated the room with its mantel of pink marble, but it was the objects on the mantelpiece that caught Meredith's eye. A large fretwork clock took up a fair amount of space, and on either side stood the statuette of a horse, rearing up on its hind legs. They looked to be an exact replica of the one Meredith had found on the floor of the Lewis's bedroom.

"I'm pleased to make your acquaintance."

Mrs. Pettigrew's voice snatched Meredith's attention away from the fireplace. The woman's high cheekbones added to her delicate features, and her light blue eyes were framed by the longest lashes Meredith had ever seen. Her mouth was full and lush, inviting even without smiling.

"Likewise, I'm sure," Meredith murmured. If George Lewis had indeed rejected this lovely creature's advances, then he must have been a man of strong principles and honor. Which didn't seem at all the manner of an embezzler.

Mrs. Pettigrew beckoned her to an elegant Queen Anne chair, then sat down herself. "I understand you wish to discuss an important matter with me?"

"Yes, thank you." Meredith sat on the chair, feeling decidedly dowdy in this woman's presence.

"May I offer you some refreshment?"

"That is very kind of you, thank you, but I must decline. I am rather short of time."

"Perhaps another time then." The widow gave her a keen glance. "To what, then, do I owe this visit?"

Meredith cleared her throat. "I came to ask you about a mutual acquaintance, the late Mr. George Lewis."

She had watched the widow's face closely, but her expression remained quite bland. "Oh, yes," she said, lifting a languid hand to pat her hair. "The manager of the bank in the High Street in Witcheston. I remember him."

Her tone was so undoubtedly without interest that Meredith felt compelled to ask, "You are aware that the Lewis family perished in a house fire a short while ago?"

Mrs. Pettigrew's eyes were cold as they regarded her. "Yes, I did hear word of it. Such a tragedy."

She might just as well have been discussing the weather. For someone who had so earnestly pursued the object of her affections, the woman seemed remarkably composed about his death.

Disturbed by the widow's apparent lack of sympathy, Meredith struggled on. "Are you also aware that Mr. Lewis was embezzling funds from the bank?"

If she had hoped to shock the woman into showing some sign of emotion, she was disappointed. Mrs. Pettigrew smoothed out a crease in her skirt. "I really don't concern myself with the town gossips, Mrs. Llewellyn. I invariably find that rumors are grossly exaggerated."

"I understand that this particular rumor has some merit." Meredith looked her in the eye. "I was wondering if perhaps you could enlighten me as to why Mr. Lewis would find it necessary to embezzle money from his bank."

For the first time something flickered in the cold eyes. "Really, Mrs. Llewellyn, I can't imagine why you would begin to think that I would be privy to that kind of information. I know nothing about Mr. Lewis's private affairs. He was my bank manager, nothing more." She reached out for the silver bell rope that hung nearby and gave it a sharp tug. "My nephew had some dealings with the man, I do believe. Perhaps he can answer your somewhat irrelevant questions."

Meredith refused to back down. The woman was obviously hiding her emotions, and Meredith's instincts told her Mrs. Pettigrew could be hiding a good deal more than that—her affection for the dead man, for one thing. "My sincere apologies for any distress I might have caused you," she said quietly, "but I have good reason to make these inquiries. A great injustice has been done, and I intend to see it is put right."

Mrs. Pettigrew studied her for a long moment, until Meredith could feel her cheeks beginning to warm. "There is one thing I can tell you," she said at last. "I do not believe that Mr. Lewis was capable of criminal activity. He was—" She broke off as the doors opened to reveal the butler.

"You rang, madam?"

"Yes, Chester. Would you please have my nephew join us at once. I believe he is in the library."

"Yes, madam."

The butler withdrew, and Meredith turned once more to the widow. "You were saying, Mrs. Pettigrew?"

To her intense disappointment, the woman's expression was once again frozen in indifference. "I was saying nothing, Mrs. Llewellyn. I'm sorry I'm unable to enlighten you. Perhaps my nephew will be more accommodating."

The doors swung open again before Meredith could think of a suitable answer. The young man who strolled in wore the same bored expression as his aunt. Dressed in a dark maroon smoking jacket and white cravat, he sported a monocle in one eye and carried a lit cigar.

Mrs. Pettigrew introduced her. "My nephew, Will Barnard." She gave the young man a meaningful look that wasn't lost on Meredith. "Mrs. Llewellyn would like a word with you before she leaves."

In other words, Meredith thought wryly, get rid of her. Well, she wasn't about to be dismissed quite so easily. "I won't take up too much of your time," she said, giving Will Barnard her brightest smile.

He sent his aunt a wary glance.

"Mrs. Llewellyn seems to believe that we have information about George Lewis's private affairs," Mrs. Pettigrew said. "I have assured her I have no such knowledge and cannot help her. Since you have had dealings with the man, perhaps you can answer her questions."

Her nephew shifted his gaze back to Meredith. "I really don't know if I will be of any help. I barely knew the man."

"Well, then, in that case, perhaps you would be so good as to escort Mrs. Llewellyn to the front door." Mrs. Pettigrew gave Meredith another of her chilling glances. "If you will excuse me. I feel a headache beginning."

"Oh, of course." Having been thoroughly dismissed, there was nothing Meredith could do but follow Barnard to the doors. As he opened them, she turned back to the widow. "I do hope your health will shortly improve, Mrs. Pettigrew."

"Thank you, Mrs. Llewellyn. I hope you eventually

find an answer to your questions." Her expression most certainly portrayed the opposite.

Not that Meredith could blame her. Mrs. Pettigrew obviously would not want her pursuit of George Lewis to be public knowledge. Apparently George had told his wife about it, who had then related the news to Amanda, but it seemed unlikely that the knowledge had gone any further than that.

Will Barnard led her down the hallway without comment, but she was determined to persuade the young man to at least consider answering her questions.

"You live in a beautiful home," she told him as they reached the front door. "Quite magnificent. The drawing room is so elegant, and I adore those horses on the mantelpiece. Staffordshire, aren't they?"

Will shrugged. "I have no idea. I don't pay attention to my aunt's furnishings. I do know they are worth a great deal of money. They are one pair of a very limited edition. Actually, George Lewis also had a pair of them in his home."

She waited until he had opened the door, and then turned to him with a smile. "I understand you take care of Mrs. Pettigrew's business at the bank."

Will pulled a face. "Not exactly. I keep the paperwork, but my aunt prefers to visit the bank personally and alone." He hesitated, then added, "At least she used to, that is."

"Until Mr. Lewis passed on."

A flicker of wariness crossed his face. "Precisely. Not that it's any of my business." *Or yours*, his expression added.

"You must have heard, I assume, that Mr. Lewis had been embezzling funds from the bank."

Will's cool gray eyes were devoid of emotion when he looked at her. "Actually, no, I didn't know. I don't suppose it matters now, does it, since the man is dead."

"Such a tragedy." Meredith busied herself pulling up her gloves to her elbows. "A great loss, the whole family dying out like that. First the mother, father, and baby, and then that little girl dying all alone. So very sad."

Will shrugged. "I suppose. These things happen. I hardly

knew the man, and never met his family, so I can't really say."

"They had such a lovely home. It's completely ruined now, of course."

"Is it? I wouldn't know. I don't even know where it is." He stepped outside and pushed the door open wider, indicating quite clearly that she should leave.

Meredith decided she didn't like this indifferent young man very much. She needed to tolerate his company a little longer, however, if she were to find out a little more about the late George Lewis.

"I noticed a motor car in the driveway when I got out of the carriage." She gave him her brightest smile. "Is it yours?"

"It is, indeed." For a moment his expression took on a more affable look. "A recent gift from my aunt."

"My goodness." Meredith turned to take another look at the shiny bright red motor car. "You have a most generous aunt." She turned back just in time to see a hint of resentment in his face.

"Actually it was in payment for . . . ah . . . a spot of business that I took care of for her."

Meredith studied his face with interest. "That must have been quite an extensive effort on your part to earn such a remarkable compensation."

The look on his face told her he regretted having disclosed so much information. She would get no more out of him.

She was proved right when Will said brusquely, "Well, good day, Mrs. Llewellyn. Thank you for calling."

Retracing her steps to where Reggie waited with the carriage, she wondered about the mysterious business matter Will Barnard had taken care of for his aunt, one that had resulted in such a generous gift. Blanche Pettigrew, with her beauty and wealth, could not be accustomed to rejection. Having been so thoroughly scorned by George Lewis, had she taken her revenge on him by ordering her nephew to burn down his house?

Neither Blanche nor Will had shown the least remorse over the tragic deaths of the Lewis family. It was certainly a possibility. Especially so, in light of Will's interesting comments about the horses. For how could he know that George Lewis had a pair of them in his home if Will had never been inside it?

It was an interesting question, and one worth pursuing, if she could only work out exactly how to do that.

Chapter 12

"I wonder what the suffragettes have got planned next." Olivia stood looking out of the kitchen window, her pensive expression drawing a frown.

"You'd better not let Mrs. Wilkins hear you mention suffragettes." Grace dragged a large china platter out of the soapy water in the sink and laid it on the draining board. "She said she didn't want to hear one mention of the word or she'd box our ears."

Olivia sniffed. "I don't know how we're supposed to be members of the WSPU if we can't get days off to go and protest. I didn't even manage to break any windows the last time we went. That bobby chucked me in the wagon before I had a chance to throw one rock."

"Just be glad I got you out of there." Grace shuddered. "I hate to think what they would have done to you in prison." Grace didn't say so, but she was jolly glad they couldn't join the protestors again for a while. So far their attempts to support the suffragettes had brought them nothing but trouble.

Olivia picked up the platter and started drying it with her tea towel. "Yeah, it would have been quite an experience.

Think of all the stories I would have heard, though, from the other women prisoners."

"If they'd been able to talk." Grace lifted a delicate bone china soup tureen out of the water. "It would be a bit hard, wouldn't it, with a flipping tube stuck down their throats."

Olivia sighed. "I s'pose so. In any case, we won't be able to go protesting until we get that blinking attic cleaned up. That's going to take us weeks."

"No it won't." Grace waited for Olivia to put the platter on the table, then handed her the tureen. "We got a lot done already."

"Yeah, I s'pose." Olivia started wiping the tureen, once more staring out the window. "Anyhow, I got a wedding dress out of it, didn't I." She turned the tureen over. "I wonder what else we'll find up there."

"Whatever we find up there we'd better leave it alone." Grace swished her hands around in the water and came up with a china jug. "I still say that wedding dress will bring you bad luck."

"Well, I'm not superstitious, so there. I don't believe in bad luck." Olivia turned to put the tureen on the table. The platter took up too much room, though, so she had to scoot it over with her elbow to put the tureen down.

As she nudged the platter out of the way, the tureen slipped from her hand. She tried to grab it, missed, and the heavy dish crashed to the floor, splintering tiny pieces of china all across the red tiles.

Grace stared in horror at the mess on the floor. "Blimey," she muttered, "now you've gone and done it."

Olivia's cheeks were pale as she stared down at the shattered china. "Gawd, that was our best bit of bone china. Wilky will have my hide for this."

Feeling sick, Grace gaped at the mess. "See?" she muttered. "I told you that dress was bad luck."

Later that afternoon in the teacher's lounge, Meredith recounted the details of her visit to the Sandalwood

Estate while Essie drank in every word and Felicity pretended not to be interested.

Essie's eyes widened when Meredith speculated on the possibility of Will Barnard setting the fire in the Lewises' house. "Do you really think he was the one?" she said, her hands clasped at her chin. "What are you going to do about it?"

Meredith uttered an unhappy sigh. "I don't think there's anything I can do about it. Every time I think I'm getting somewhere, I realize I can't prove anything. It's all ifs and maybes. The constables are not going to arrest anyone on such nebulous evidence."

"I suppose not." Essie sighed with her. "It's terrible to think he might have got away with the murder of three people. Especially that little baby."

"If you ask me," Felicity said, raising her head from the book on her lap, "you are wasting your time, Meredith. Obviously you are getting nowhere, and sooner or later Hamilton is going to find out what you're doing. I hate to think how he'll react to that. Especially when you tell him you're doing it for a ghost."

Essie gasped. "Oh, you couldn't possibly tell him that, Meredith."

Meredith smiled. "Don't worry, Essie. I have no intention of telling Mr. Hamilton about my ghost. I do wish I knew where to go from here, though. Emma is going to be so disappointed in me."

"She can't be disappointed," Felicity murmured, her head down over her book again. "Ghosts don't have feelings."

"If you'd seen the tears on her face, you wouldn't say that." Meredith picked up her knitting and began clicking her needles in rapid rhythm. "I can't get that vision out of my mind."

"She cries? Oh, my." Essie buried her face in her hands. "That would break my heart."

"The tears aren't real, either. The child is dead."

Meredith frowned. She was used to Felicity's blunt

manner, but sometimes it rankled. "She was alive until a few days ago," she said crisply.

Felicity sounded exasperated. "All I can say is that if there really is a ghost, it's certainly causing a lot of trouble for a child who's no longer with us. Give it up, Meredith, before you land us all in trouble."

Meredith lapsed into silence. She couldn't give up. Not as long as that tearful face haunted her. There had to be a way to find out what really happened that night. Something, somewhere, to tell her what she needed to know.

After a lengthy silence, Felicity snapped her book shut and rose. "Well, I have to go and teach those little hooligans how to converse with French nobility. Though when they will ever need to use it, goodness only knows. I should be teaching them how to invade the London men's clubs and set fire to their nasty little derrieres."

Essie gasped. "Felicity! How could you!"

"I only wish I could." Felicity waved a hand at them both and sailed out the door.

Meredith gave Essie a wry grin. "Felicity will never change, I'm afraid. She will always be a rebel at heart." She tucked her knitting away in its bag and got to her feet. "I must get back to my office. I still have all that cash we raised at the summer fete in the safe. I really should take it to the bank and open up an account now that we've started a new art studio fund."

Essie scrambled up from her chair. "I think a new art studio is such a good idea. I'm so glad the school board supported it."

"Yes, but it's not safe to leave money lying around like that. Too much of a temptation. I should have thought of it when I went to the bank in Witcheston. It will be some time, I'm afraid, before we raise enough money to add the new studio."

"You certainly need another one. Your classroom is so cramped for space, you hardly have room for the easels."

"Which is why we must hold all these fund-raising

events. I should have asked Mr. Hamilton for a new art studio instead of another horse."

Essie stared at her. "You asked for another horse? Is something wrong with Major?"

"Other than the fact he is getting too old to go far these days, no. I just don't like to overburden him."

"Poor Major." Essie started for the door. "It's a good job we don't have to go into town too often."

"It is, indeed." Though, Meredith thought, as she headed for her office, if ghosts kept appearing in her bedroom demanding justice, she might end up spending more time traveling around the countryside than in the classroom. She could just imagine what Stuart Hamilton would say to that.

Arriving at her office, she found Roger Platt seated at her desk, reading something he obviously didn't want her to see, since he hastily folded the magazine and tucked it inside his coat.

"Mrs. Llewellyn!" He shoved the chair back and jumped to his feet. "I didn't realize you were back. I thought you were still gallivanting around town with the handyman."

He'd made it sound insulting, and Meredith longed to slap him. "I completed my urgent business earlier than I expected." Glaring into his eyes, she added, "I trust you completed the proposals for the next fund-raiser?"

He looked blank for a moment, then said hurriedly, "I was just getting to it, m'm. I'll finish it in the library. It should be quiet in there now."

"Good. And please refrain from your questionable reading material until your work is done."

He had the grace to look sheepish. "Yes, m'm. Sorry, m'm." Gathering up two of the ledgers, he rushed past her and out the door.

Sighing, she took her seat behind the desk. Papers and notebooks lay scattered all over the surface, covering up the inkwell and blotter. With a frown, she began tidying them up, placing them in a neat pile on one side of the desk.

Coming across a page torn from a notebook, she glanced at it before throwing it into the wastebasket. Doodles covered the whole page. Peering at them, she saw that they were sketches of young women, all clothed in their undergarments.

Clicking her tongue, Meredith dropped the offending page into the basket. It was really too bad that Mr. Platt wasted what appeared to be a halfway decent artistic talent on such scandalous scribbling. She really would have to take a sterner hand to that young man.

Having tidied the desk to her satisfaction, she rose and walked over to the file cabinet. A small safe sat on top of it, and she quickly dialed the code to open it.

Two stacks of pound notes lay inside, and she pulled them out, then closed the door of the safe and spun the dial. Arriving back at her desk, she pulled off the rubber bands, then began to count the notes.

She had barely begun when a chill drifted across the back of her neck. Pausing, she stared at the crumpled notes in her hand. Surely not.

True, Kathleen's ghost had appeared in other places, such as the flower gardens and even once in her classroom, but then Kathleen was well acquainted with the school. Emma was not. So far, apart from that brief glimpse at the orphanage, she had only appeared in Meredith's room. She couldn't possibly have found her way to the office.

Slowly, Meredith lifted her head. She could see nothing but the pale green walls of the office, the cream gauze curtains at the window, the dark green carpet. No shadowy figure hovered in front of the bookcase or drifted around the chairs.

Relaxing her shoulders, Meredith decided she had imagined that cold draft. Having lost count of the notes, she began counting them again.

Once more a breath of frigid air brushed her neck. At the same time, she felt icy fingers touch her hand. Startled, she jerked her chin up, and stared straight into the face of Emma Lewis.

With a sharp cry, Meredith pushed her chair back so hard she crashed into the wall. It was the first time she'd come that close to the ghost. It was not a comfortable experience.

Her sudden movement must have frightened the child, as the vision had vanished, leaving not even a whisper of mist in its place.

Angry at her lack of composure, Meredith looked around the room. "Emma? I'm sorry. You startled me, that's all. I need to speak with you. Please, come back."

Only the suddenly loud ticking of her clock answered her. Frustrated, Meredith once more began counting the pound notes from the beginning.

She had almost finished when she became aware of the tingling all the way down her arms where her skin had risen in tiny bumps. The room had grown uncommonly cold. Bracing herself, she slowly raised her head.

The misty cloud hovered just a few feet away, Emma's face only vaguely visible in the center. One ghostly hand pointed straight at the desk.

Frowning, Meredith swept her gaze over the desk's surface. She could see nothing on it but the papers and notebooks, three ledgers, the inkstand with the inkwell and penholder, the blotter, and the pound notes she still held in her hand.

She looked back at Emma, who seemed to be fading into the mist. "No, wait! I don't understand. What is it you are trying to tell me?"

Emma's finger pointed straight at her.

Meredith looked down at her bodice. She wore no brooch today, no pendant. Just a white shirtwaist with her blue serge skirt. "I'm sorry, I—"

She broke off as the ghostly finger once more jabbed at her, lower this time. Looking down at her hands, Meredith said slowly, "The money? Are you pointing at the money? Why would you need money?" She looked up, alarmed to see Emma had almost disappeared.

With a pang of dismay, Meredith realized her worst

fears had materialized. The fragile thread of communication between them was gradually growing weaker. Either Emma's strength was failing, or she was losing her own tenuous powers.

She raised her hand in appeal. "Wait! You must help me. Is it the money? We raised it at the summer fete. It's for a new art studio. I'm taking it to the bank tomorrow . . ." She caught her breath as the mist glowed for an instant, and Emma's face looked out at her, her blue eyes wide and beseeching.

"The bank." Meredith peered intently at the hazy figure. "This has something to do with the bank."

The cloud vanished so suddenly she blinked. The room grew warm again. Emma had gone.

Looking down at the money in her hands, Meredith tried hard to concentrate. What could any of this possibly have to do with the bank? George Lewis was no longer there. Unless it had something to do with his embezzling.

That must be it. She had thought all along that the fire had something to do with George's embezzling. This was what Emma was trying to tell her. But how did that help her? She still knew no more than she had before. She needed more information.

Her gaze fell on the folded newspaper she'd laid on the corner of her desk earlier. With a tinge of excitement she reached for it.

Of course. She should have thought of it before. She needed to read the reports on the fire to see if there was anything there that might help her.

The old newspapers and magazines were kept in the coal shed, used to light the fireplace fires. They had been piling up all summer, and only recently had the fires been lit to warm the rooms. There might be a slim chance that the newspaper with news of the Lewis fire was still there.

Without wasting another moment, Meredith thrust the money back into the safe and hurried from the room.

On her way down the corridor she came face to face

with Sylvia Montrose. Hoping to avoid a delay, she gave her a brief nod and would have passed her by had Sylvia not stepped in front of her, barring her path.

"Oh, there you are, Meredith. I was just on my way to see you."

Inwardly cursing the interruption to her plans, Meredith forced a smile. "I hope it's not anything untoward?"

"Well, I suppose that depends." Sylvia's lisp seemed more pronounced, and she appeared to be quite agitated.

Meredith's heart sank. "On what?"

"On whether or not you consider a gross misrepresentation of facts to be a transgression."

Meredith frowned. "I'm afraid I don't understand."

"I'm talking about Felicity Cross. What, pray, is she thinking when she instructs her students to refuse to curtsy to French notables? Is she attempting to spark another Hundred Years' War?"

Meredith bit her lip. "I hardly think Miss Cross has any such ambitions. I really can't comment on her remarks without hearing the entire conversation. I will, however, have a word with her, if that will satisfy you?"

Sylvia gave her a look full of suspicion. "I hope you will sternly rebuke her. I should hate to be obliged to speak to Mr. Hamilton about this."

"I can assure you, I will get to the bottom of the matter." With great difficulty Meredith refrained from adding a derisive comment about Sylvia's passion for protocol. "You can safely leave the matter with me."

"I certainly hope so." She gave Meredith a sly look. "I know how fond you are of Miss Cross. I hope it won't prejudice your judgment of her behavior."

"Most emphatically not." *Not that it's any of your business*, she added inwardly. The woman really was an insufferable prig. It was no wonder Felicity hated her so.

"Well, good. Then I shall refrain from complaining to Mr. Hamilton for the time being." Her tone suggested she would take great pleasure in tattling to Hamilton at the slightest opportunity.

Meredith pulled a face at Sylvia's retreating back, then continued on her way to the coal shed.

Inside the shed the smell of coal dust threatened to choke her, and she carried a stack of newspapers outside, where she could breathe in the cool autumn air.

Seated on the stone border that separated the courtyard from the gardens, she quickly sorted through the copies of the *Witcheston Post*. Since the account had been on the front page, it didn't take her long to find the one she wanted.

There it was, the picture of the Lewis house, flames leaping into the night sky. The story of the family who had lost their lives followed underneath, and Meredith eagerly scanned the lines.

She had read the story earlier, when it had first come out, although she remembered few of the details. Here was the account of the little girl found trapped in a tree outside her blazing window. Of course she remembered now.

Skimming through the story, however, brought no significant information to light. Most of the report contained what she already knew, the details garishly exaggerated by the overly enthusiastic reporter.

Vastly disappointed, Meredith returned the rest of the newspapers to the shed. She was so tired of hitting a brick wall. If only she knew for certain that she was on the right track, these setbacks would be easier to bear. Even Emma and her desperate signals had failed to assure her of that.

Yet somehow she could not let go of the conviction that the answers lay out there, and if she searched diligently enough, she would eventually find them. That, and the vision of a child's tears, was all that kept her going.

Chapter 13

Returning to the main building, Meredith headed straight for the teacher's lounge. As she had expected, Felicity and Essie were already there, and a sulky-faced Sylvia sat in the corner. Judging by the distress on Essie's face and the flush of Felicity's cheeks, words must have been exchanged between the latter and Sylvia Montrose.

A tense silence hung in the room as Meredith entered, and Essie implored her with her eyes to settle whatever dispute had arisen.

Felicity refused to look up, pretending an interest in her book, betrayed by the fact that she hadn't yet turned the first page.

Meredith sat in her favorite chair and laid the newspaper on the table in front of her. "It has turned rather chilly, don't you think?" she said, fixing Felicity with a meaningful look.

Felicity, her gaze focused on her book, didn't answer her.

"I think Meredith is addressing you, Felicity," Essie said, giving her a nudge that nearly sent the book flying off Felicity's lap.

Felicity looked up, resentment burning in her eyes. "Oh, there you are, Meredith. I was wondering what had kept you."

"Is something wrong?"

"Nothing at all." Felicity threw a burning glance in Sylvia's direction. "Not unless you take into account Miss Montrose's objections to my teaching methods, none of which are any of her business, by the way."

Sylvia's chin shot up. "I beg to differ, Miss Cross. It is indeed my business when your methods are in direct conflict to the good manners I am attempting to instill in these young ladies. I work hard to accomplish my objectives, and at every turn your outlandish tutelage sets me back. I'm beginning to think you are deliberately sabotaging my efforts for some obscure reason."

Felicity's scowl grew darker with every word of Sylvia's speech. "Outlandish? How dare you, madam! I'll have you know my methods have been approved by renowned professors of both Oxford and Cambridge."

Sylvia sniffed. "Women, I presume."

Felicity's mouth tightened. "You have something against women teachers, Miss Montrose? How odd, since I was under the impression you are one yourself. Or perhaps I was mistaken?"

Sylvia soared to her feet, her cheeks flaming. "I do not have to take such insubordination from a troublemaker whose behavior is a distinct detriment to the well-being and future of Bellehaven pupils. Mr. Hamilton shall hear of this, I promise you." With that, she swept across the room and out of the door.

Meredith groaned. "Felicity, you are incorrigible. Now I'll be forced to defend you against Stuart Hamilton's caustic comments."

The fire in Felicity's eyes slowly faded. "Bosh, Meredith. You know you enjoy sparring with Hamilton. You even go so far as to encourage it at times."

Meredith felt her cheeks grow warm. "I do not enjoy

sparring with anyone, Felicity. Especially you. Is it true you urged your students not to pay homage to French nobility?"

Felicity shrugged. "It's of no consequence. You know as well as I do that French titles have been coming and going since the Revolution. There are few nobles left in France, and they are highly unlikely to make the acquaintance of our little darlings."

"Even so, it might have been wiser to refrain from such a highly prejudiced dictum."

"I suppose you're right. The students were getting restless and I needed something a little preposterous to get their attention." She grinned. "I must say, they heartily approved of the edict."

"Of course they would."

"I do hope you won't be in trouble with Mr. Hamilton," Essie said, her face creased in concern. "I should hate to see you lose your position over something so trivial."

"Oh, I'm not in the least worried." Felicity sent Meredith a sly look. "I'm quite sure Meredith will placate the ogre. She has quite a knack of smoothing his ruffled feathers and restoring his good humor. I really think he has taken a fancy to you, Meredith."

"Stuff and nonsense. Mr. Hamilton is and always has been interested only in business matters. He is dedicated to the smooth running of this school, and that is the only reason for his visits. So you can put aside any notion of personal interest." Her cheeks hot, Meredith sought a distraction. "I found this newspaper. It has the account of the Lewis house fire."

Her smile fading, Felicity took the newspaper from her. "I remember the day this story came out. I sat reading it at the railway station while I waited for the new batch of supplies to arrive on the London train. If you remember, I spent most of the day there before the stationmaster told me there had been a derailment and there would be no trains from London until the next day." She shook her head.

"Such a waste of time. I don't know why it took so long for the message to reach him."

Essie said something that Meredith didn't hear. She was too busy pursuing the thoughts running through her head. For some reason Felicity's words had rung a bell, though she couldn't quite grasp the significance.

"Don't you think, Meredith?"

Essie's voice roused her from her musing. "I beg your pardon, Essie?"

"I said, it's such a shame you couldn't help that poor child. I simply hate to think of her wandering all alone out there, just longing to be with her family."

It was on the tip of Meredith's tongue to tell Essie she had seen the ghost a few minutes earlier in her office, but caution prevailed. It would be best if she didn't mention the ghost again, until she had something more substantial to offer.

Thinking of Emma reminded her of the pound notes that had captured the child's attention. "I'll be taking the carriage to town again tomorrow," she announced. "I must take the money we raised at the summer fete and deposit it in the bank. I'll open up a special account for the art studio."

"That is a sound idea."

Meredith glanced at the other woman. "I was wondering, Felicity, if you would mind keeping an eye on my class in the morning. I will set the tasks, but I'll need someone to supervise and make sure the students complete their assignments."

"As long as you don't expect me to paint something." Felicity yawned, and stretched her feet out one at a time. "As you well know, I have trouble drawing a straight line."

Meredith smiled. "All you'll have to do is sit at my desk and read. I'll have the assignments written on the blackboard."

"I think I can manage that." She looked up. "Are you sure you want to trust me with your students? You're not afraid I'll lead them down the path to destruction?"

"I'd trust you with my life," Meredith assured her. Although secretly she wished Felicity would use a little more restraint. She wasn't looking forward to another confrontation with Stuart Hamilton.

The following morning she left early for her journey to Witcheston. The sun shone brightly in a clear blue sky, and Reggie was in high spirits. Even Major seemed a little more energetic, and they arrived in the town in record time.

Carrying the pound notes carefully concealed in her handbag, Meredith entered the bank and went directly to the counter. This time she was the sole customer, and was served immediately by the smiling clerk, who informed her that Howard Clark was away on business.

He assured her, however, that he could open an account for her. "I'm also the assistant manager," he told her. "Desmond White, at your service. I took over from Mr. Clark when he took George Lewis's position."

"Thank you. I really didn't want to carry all this money back to the school." Meredith emptied the pound notes onto the counter.

"My, that is a lot of notes." The clerk gathered them up and expertly flipped through the corners to count them. "I make it forty-three pounds. Is that right?"

"Quite right." Meredith smiled at him. "Were you acquainted with Mr. Lewis?"

"Indeed, I was." The clerk looked around as if making sure he could not be overheard. "Very nice gentleman, Mr. Lewis. I was shocked to learn how he'd died. The whole family, too. Terrible." He stacked the notes together and snapped a rubber band around them.

Meredith hesitated, then decided she had nothing to lose. She might as well explore every avenue open to her. She leaned forward and said quietly, "You must have been even more shocked to learn he'd embezzled money."

Desmond looked up. "George? No, there had to be some mistake there. I never believed it, anyway. George Lewis was an honest, upright man. I can't believe he would take money that wasn't his. Now, if it had been Mr. Clark, I'd be more inclined to believe that. Shifty, I call him. He spends money like it's water. You'd think he was a blinking millionaire to hear him talk, if you'll pardon my language."

Meredith raised her eyebrows. "Mr. Clark is wealthy?"

The clerk shrugged. "I don't know about that. Though he's always bragging about the things he's bought. Jewelry, fancy clothes, nice things for the house. I think he's trying to catch up with the way George Lewis lived. Always jealous of George, he was." He leaned forward and lowered his voice. "George's wife was the one with the money. Came from a good family, she did. It was her house they lived in, I'm told."

"I take it from your tone that you don't much care for Mr. Clark."

"That I don't. He's always complaining, nothing I can ever do pleases him. I really miss George." He straightened, opened a drawer in front of him, and took out a new passbook. Writing down an account number inside the first page, he added, "George always treated the staff like they were family. Good worker, too. He was working late the last day he was here. Said he had an important appointment the next morning and wanted to make up the time. Not many blokes would do that. Especially when they're the manager and don't have to answer to no one but themselves." He shook his head. "I remember that last day. He was acting strange, like he was really worried about something."

Meredith leaned forward. "Did he say what the appointment was, or with whom?"

To her disappointment, Desmond shook his head. "No, he didn't. I got the impression it was something he wanted kept secret." He handed Meredith the passbook. "There you are, Mrs. Llewellyn. All taken care of. Your money is safe and sound now."

"Thank you, Mr. White."

"My pleasure, m'm, I'm sure."

Meredith tucked the passbook in her handbag. "I suppose Mr. Lewis kept an appointment book?"

Desmond stared at her, one hand wandering to his tie. "Er . . . well, yes, I suppose, but . . ."

She smiled at him. "I realize this isn't quite protocol, Mr. White, but if I tell you that it's extremely important I know where Mr. Lewis intended to go the morning after he died, would you perhaps permit me a quick peek at his appointment book?"

Desmond narrowed his eyes. "I'm not exactly sure if it's still here."

"Could you at least take a look for me?"

Still he hesitated, while she held her breath. She had tried so hard to find out why George Lewis had needed money desperately enough to steal it. This mysterious appointment might just answer that question.

After a long, tense pause, Desmond gave her a quick nod. "I'll take a look. It's probably with the rest of his things. They're packed in a box waiting for someone to pick them up."

He disappeared through a door behind him, and emerged a moment later with a black book in his hand. "Here it is. Don't know if it will tell you what you want to know, though."

Quickly, Meredith thumbed through the pages until she reached the last entry. There it was, printed in a neat hand across the page. *Ten o'clock. Meeting with Inspector Edward Dawson of the Witcheston Constabulary.*

Meredith swallowed, then handed the book back to the curious clerk. "Thank you, Mr. White. I appreciate your cooperation. There's no need to mention this to anyone else." *Especially Howard Clark*, she added inwardly.

Desmond briefly placed a finger against his lips. "Mum's the word, m'm."

"By the way, do you happen to know where Mr. Clark went today?"

"Yes, I do, m'm. He went to London for a meeting at our main branch. Won't be back until tomorrow."

Meredith's jaw dropped as she stared at him. Now she remembered why Felicity's words had rung a bell.

Desmond's face focused in front of her and she realized she was still staring at him. "Er . . . I was actually thinking of calling on Mrs. Clark," she said hurriedly. "Could you give me her address?"

Obviously baffled, Desmond wrote the address down on a piece of paper and handed it to her. "I don't know what's going on," he said quietly, "but if you need my help for anything, just let me know."

Caught up in her excitement, she nodded her thanks and hurried from the bank.

George Lewis had intended to meet with a police inspector. Was it to confess his own guilt, or to accuse someone else of the embezzlement? Someone such as Howard Clark, for instance.

Howard had told her that he'd returned from London the day after the fire. Which he couldn't have done, since Felicity had waited all afternoon for a train that never came. Had Howard simply made a mistake in the day, or had he deliberately lied about going to London in order to establish an alibi?

It was certainly a possibility. But that's all she had. Possibilities, suspects, theories, but no proof of anything.

"Where to now, m'm?" Reggie asked when she had returned to the carriage.

She handed him the piece of paper. "Do you know where that is?"

He frowned at the address in his hand. "Not sure, m'm, but I'll find it." He helped her up into the carriage. "Do you know who set the fire yet, m'm?"

"Not yet, Reggie. But I do believe I'm getting closer."

His eyes sparkled with excitement. "You'll let me in on it when you know, right, m'm?"

"Of course I will." She settled back on her seat, wondering if she'd ever know for sure.

The journey to Howard Clark's house was a short one. The cottage sat at the very edge of the town on a beech-shaded lane. Its thatched roof dipped low over latticed windows, and purple and gold chrysanthemums still bloomed in the front yard.

Reggie halted the carriage at the gate and helped her down. "Want me to come with you, m'm?" he asked hopefully, and seemed disappointed when she declined.

"I shan't be but a moment," she assured him, and tramped up the garden path, her feet scrunching on the gravel.

A disgruntled-looking housekeeper showed her into the parlor, and a few minutes later Sophie Clark entered the room. She was a thin-faced woman of middle age, with sad eyes and lines of discontent dragging down her mouth at the corners.

She seemed disinclined to listen as Meredith explained she was from Bellehaven and needed volunteers to help with the Christmas pageant. "I realize it's more than two months away," she said, determined to hold on to the woman's attention, "but it's never too early to ask for help."

Sophie regarded her with a sour look. "What brought you to my house, may I ask?"

Meredith crossed her fingers behind her back. "I happened to be at the bank and overheard someone mentioning your extraordinary talent in organizing such events. I just had to come and ask you to give us the benefit of your experience."

Sophie wore the stunned look of someone being honored for a false accomplishment. She began stuttering. "Well, I . . . don't know what to say . . . I can't imagine who . . . I mean—"

Although the cottage was far more modest than the Lewis home, the furnishings in the parlor were of the highest quality. Fine china vases sat on a lovely oak sideboard, oil paintings graced the walls, while two Chippendale armchairs accompanied an elegant cream brocade settee that must have cost a small fortune.

Desmond White hadn't exaggerated Howard Clark's

spending spree, Meredith reflected as she eyed the lush Axminster carpet.

"My," she murmured, "you certainly have a beautiful home."

Sophie's attitude was improving considerably from Meredith's flattery, and she now seemed eager to entertain. "Howard—my husband—has been most generous." She sat on the edge of the settee as if afraid it would break.

"It all looks so new." Meredith sniffed the air. "I do so love the smell of new furniture."

"Yes, it is. Quite new, I mean." Sophie picked up a small fan and began waving it in front of her face. "My husband recently came into an inheritance. An aunt of his died and left him a large sum of money." Her laugh sounded forced. "Most unexpected, I must say. Howard had made no mention of her until then. He couldn't imagine why she should name him in her will. It just goes to show, one never knows what will happen next."

"Yes, indeed." Meredith folded her hands in her lap. The inheritance was entirely possible, of course. Then again, the woman could be lying, or perhaps speaking what she thought was the truth. If Howard was guilty of embezzling, he wasn't likely to tell his wife.

If only she could take a look at the bank's records. She'd had enough experience with accounting to be able to spot discrepancies if they were there.

"Would you like some tea?"

Meredith started at Sophie's voice. "Oh, thank you, but I must get back to the school." She rose, anxious to put her next plan into action. "Perhaps another time?"

"Oh, yes, do call again. I don't get many visitors. It's not much use having fine things to show off if there's no one to show them to, is it. I don't get out that much and Howard is always gone somewhere. He's in London today, at a bank meeting."

Meredith paused on her way to the door. "Does he have to do that often? Go to London on business, I mean."

Sophie sent her an odd look. "Not very often, no. Maybe twice a year."

"Oh, so he wasn't in London about two months ago?"

The woman's expression grew even more puzzled. "No, not that I know of."

Meredith nodded. "Well, thank you for your time, Mrs. Clark."

"It was a great pleasure meeting you, Mrs. Llewellyn. And you can count on me to help with the pageant."

Meredith had completely forgotten her excuse for calling and tripped over her next words. "That was . . . er . . . is so good of you . . . I . . . we appreciate your help."

"Not at all. I shall look forward to it."

Meredith heard the door close behind her with a sense of relief. She wasn't at all experienced in fabricating stories and making excuses. It didn't come easy to her and she regretted having to stoop to such levels to find out the truth.

As it was, she still didn't have all the answers. So far she had two viable suspects. Howard Clark had come into money, and had lied about his trip to London, but that could have been for any number of reasons.

As for Blanche Pettigrew's nephew, Will Barnard, he knew more about the Lewis house than he was willing to admit, and he'd been amply rewarded for a task he had performed for his aunt. But that didn't make him guilty of murder.

Reggie greeted her with a question in his voice, and she had to shake her head at him in defeat. She was no closer to discovering who had set the fire in the Lewis home, or even establishing the fact that murder had been committed. For every step she took forward, she fell two steps back.

Staring out the window at the wheat fields flowing past, she thought about her short conversation with Sophie Clark. There was only one thing left to do.

Somehow she had to get her hands on those bank

records and find out if Howard Clark had a stronger motive than jealousy to kill his manager. If so, she would take the evidence to the inspector herself, and put the entire matter into his hands.

Chapter 14

On the ride home Meredith's head hurt with trying to work out the problem of how she would gain access to the bank records. She would have to enlist the help of her friends, that much was certain.

Arriving back at the school, she was relieved to find both Essie and Felicity in the teacher's lounge, with no sign of Sylvia Montrose.

Felicity gave her an account of the class she'd taken for her. "Your students were remarkably well behaved," she told Meredith as she settled herself on her chair. "You should be commended. They seem to have an avid interest in painting, even if the results do leave much to be desired."

Meredith sighed. "Just once I would love to have a truly talented painter in my class. Some of these girls should never be let loose with a paintbrush in their hand. Their efforts make me shudder. It is so frustrating to spend so much time teaching them how to paint when I know full well they'll never touch a paintbrush again once they leave Bellehaven."

Essie murmured a protest. "You're teaching them far

more than how to paint, Meredith dear. You're teaching them to appreciate the beauty of nature, to enjoy the magical effects of light and shade, to observe the tiny details that make up everyday objects that the untrained eye misses. Their world will be brighter, more colorful, and far more informative because of your efforts."

Felicity sniffed. "They'll be lucky if they have time to notice any of those things. They'll be too busy giving dinner parties, entertaining guests, ordering servants about, and hiring nannies and tutors for their children, not to mention time wasted rolling around in bed servicing their husbands."

Essie shrieked and threw her hands over her face.

Meredith shook her head. "Felicity Cross, for heaven's sake. You have not one jot of decorum in your entire being."

Felicity grinned. "Too bad Miss Snot isn't here. She'd have something else with which to go running to Hamilton. If she dare repeat to his face what I said."

Meredith preferred not to think of Stuart Hamilton in the context of Felicity's earlier comment. "Well, I'm relieved she isn't here. I have a favor to ask of you both, and it's not something I can allow anyone else to hear."

Essie's eyebrows twitched in nervous anticipation, while Felicity regarded her with only mild curiosity. "I suppose this has to do with your ghost," she said, sounding resigned.

"Actually it has a lot more to do with the fire at the Lewis home."

Now Felicity looked alarmed. "You're not asking us to go into that house, I hope?"

Essie uttered a tiny squeak, and Meredith shook her head. "No, no, of course not." She related her conversations with Desmond White and Sophie Clark.

"My," Felicity said when she was finished, "you have been busy. You really think this Howard Clark person might have killed the Lewis family?"

"I think it's possible." Meredith sighed. "I also think it's possible that Will Barnard might have set fire to the house on orders from his aunt. I just don't know how to prove anything."

"Simple." Felicity beamed at Essie. "We just send our beautiful young maiden here to charm Mr. Barnard into confessing his crime. One look into her eyes and he'll be babbling like a fool."

Essie tossed her head, ruffling the golden curls on her forehead. "Oh, really, Felicity. You can be quite insufferable at times."

"Oh, bosh, Essie. I was only teasing." ·

"Well, thank goodness." Essie pouted. "You know I have no stomach for entertaining a suspected murderer."

Meredith stared at her. "You know, Essie, Felicity may well be right. If anyone could get the truth out of Will Barnard, it would be you."

Essie gasped in horror, while Felicity laughed out loud. "And how, pray, will you manage to get him to confess to a murder?"

"I'm not expecting him to confess. I do want to know, however, how he knew about those horses on George Lewis's fireplace."

"Perhaps he saw a picture of them somewhere." Felicity reached for her book.

"Perhaps."

"In any case, how could you arrange a meeting between him and Essie?"

"No." Essie shook her head so violently her curls bounced on her forehead. "Absolutely not. I refuse. I simply couldn't." She glanced at Meredith. "Oh, please don't look at me like that. You know how I hate saying no to you."

"Then say yes." Meredith reached for her hand. "We will pay Mrs. Pettigrew another visit, asking for her help with the Christmas pageant. While we are there, you can engage Will Barnard in conversation, and ask him certain questions. Felicity and I would be close by, so you would not be compromised in any way."

Essie still looked doubtful. "What sort of questions?"

"That's something we will have to work out." Meredith turned to Felicity. "Can we count on you to help?"

"Well, of course." Felicity looked at both of them in turn. "I'm game for anything that gets the better of a man."

"Then it's settled." Meredith hesitated. "There is, however, something else with which I'll need your help."

Felicity groaned. "Don't tell me. You want Essie to charm a confession out of Howard Clark."

Essie shuddered. "Please, Meredith. The man sounds positively evil."

"It's all right, Essie. Howard Clark will be on a train returning from London tomorrow." Quickly she told them her idea.

Essie still looked as if she would run from the room, but Felicity applauded with gusto. "Now that's what I call an exciting morning."

"We'll make both visits tomorrow morning," Meredith told them. "We'll call on Mrs. Pettigrew, then go to the bank. Depending on what we find out, we might possibly pay a visit to Inspector Dawson in Witcheston, in the hopes that he will be able to take the matter into his own hands."

"The bank closes early on a Saturday," Essie reminded her.

Meredith nodded. "It also opens late, which is why we must go to the Sandalwood Estate first. You will have to be as swift as possible, Essie, if you are to learn anything from Mr. Barnard."

Essie's frown grew more intense.

"There's just one problem as I see it," Felicity said. "How do we explain our absence to Miss Snot?"

"I've thought about that." Meredith leaned back in her chair. "You will be accompanying me into Witcheston to decide what we shall need to purchase for the Christmas pageant. It will take us some time to compare prices, et cetera. Meanwhile, we shall need a responsible adult to take charge here and see that the students are either sensibly occupied or have permission to go into the village. I'm quite sure Sylvia will be amenable to taking on the role of supervisor."

"Excellent. You've thought of everything." Felicity rubbed her hands together. "I'm rather looking forward to this adventure. It will be fun to go into Witcheston. It's been ages since I was there."

"Well, it's time we made our way to the dining hall." Meredith gestured at the clock on the mantelpiece. "Supper is early tonight, since we have to be at the village hall by seven o'clock for the recital."

Essie jumped to her feet. "I must say, I'm looking forward to the recital tonight much more than our ventures tomorrow. What if something goes wrong? We will be in terrible trouble."

"Nothing will go wrong," Meredith promised her, sounding far more confident than she felt. "As long as we all keep precisely to our roles, we should have no problems at all."

All through the recital that evening she kept reassuring herself of that. For Essie was quite right. If all did not go as planned, they could be in deep trouble, indeed.

The recital was a resounding success, judging from the applause that kept the students on the stage for quite a while before they could finally make their exit.

By the time the entire student body had been rounded up and shepherded safely back to the school, Meredith was quite exhausted.

Upon lying down on her bed, she fell into a deep sleep almost immediately. She awoke sometime later, too drowsy to realize at first that the room had grown unnaturally cold.

Once the chill penetrated, however, she was instantly awake and shot upright, scanning the room for the green cloud. All she could see was a faint shadow moving in the corner, which could be a trick of the moonlight filtering through the gap in the curtains.

Quickly she found the lamp and lit it. Holding it above her head, she said softly, "Emma? Is that you?"

The shadow moved, and began to form into a cloud. Holding her breath, Meredith waited for the familiar face to appear. For an instant she saw it, just a pale shape, too indistinct to make out the features.

Part of the shadow moved—a hand wafting weakly in the air.

Meredith spoke again in a louder whisper. "Emma? What can you tell me?"

Even before she had finished speaking, the cloud seemed to fold up into itself and then it disappeared.

Meredith stared at the empty corner in dismay. Time was running out for her to help Emma. She was certain of that now. She had to find the answers, and soon.

She woke up in a fever of impatience the next morning, and hurried down to the dining hall to meet Essie and Felicity for breakfast.

Essie looked pale, and sat without speaking while the students chattered all around her.

Meredith noticed several of the girls sending worried glances in their beloved teacher's direction. Being the closest in age to the students of Bellehaven, normally Essie would be joining in the conversation, talking and laughing along with everyone else.

Felicity, on the other hand, seemed vibrant and in excellent spirits. Now and then Meredith heard a burst of laughter from the students at her table, no doubt in response to one of Felicity's irreverent jokes.

Sylvia Montrose, at the fourth table, was holding forth on what appeared to be a serious discussion that was obviously boring to the unlucky young women forced to listen to her.

Meredith smiled. Sylvia would enjoy her morning taking charge of everyone. She had expressed her pleased surprise when Meredith had informed her the night before, and had hastened to assure Meredith that she was quite capable of handling the duties.

As for herself, Meredith felt as if she sat on pins and needles, waiting for the moment when she could dismiss everyone. Reggie had been told to bring the carriage around to the front door precisely at nine, and it was almost that now.

There were still one or two girls who had not yet finished their meal, and three more who sat talking while their tea grew cold.

Deciding she could wait no longer, Meredith made her announcement. Rising to her feet, she tapped her saucer loudly with her spoon. She had to wait several moments for the chatter to die down, but at last she had their attention.

"Miss Cross, Miss Pickard, and myself have errands to run in Witchceston this morning," she said as a sea of faces turned expectantly in her direction. "While we are gone, Miss Montrose will be in charge."

A few faint groans answered her announcement, and were immediately hushed up by the other students. Ignoring them, Meredith continued, "Those of you who wish to go into the village will ask Miss Montrose for permission, while the rest of you will continue your usual weekend activities under her guidance."

At her signal, the students rose, muttering and murmuring as they filed out of the hall. Meredith, joined by Essie and Felicity, followed them, with Sylvia bringing up the rear.

"I still can't understand why it should take three of you to decide on purchases for the pageant," she complained as they entered the hallway. "Surely that is something you could manage by yourself, Meredith?"

Noting Sylvia's worried frown, Meredith wondered if she might be having second thoughts about being in charge. "We have a budget," she told her. "We have to hunt down the best prices possible from what is offered, and that takes time. With three of us, we can cover the whole town in one morning and be back here this afternoon."

"Well, I suppose . . ." Sylvia's voice trailed off.

Felicity gave her a sharp glance. "If you're not able to take charge of the students, Miss Montrose, I'll be happy to change places with you."

Meredith's breath froze for a moment, then puffed out

when Sylvia's chin lifted. "Of course I'm able, Miss Cross. Able and willing, in fact."

"Well, good." Felicity strode off, throwing over her shoulder, "Just don't let the little darlings take advantage of you, that's all."

Sylvia shot Meredith a worried look. "What exactly did she mean by that?"

Inwardly cursing Felicity's devilish tongue, Meredith said quickly, "Nothing at all, Sylvia. Everything will be quite all right, I'm sure of it."

"Of course it will." Still looking as if she expected the sky to fall on her any moment, Sylvia hurried off down the hallway.

Meredith suppressed a stab of guilt as she hurried after Felicity. Sylvia had to learn to take responsibility sooner or later, and weekends were usually fairly mundane. Felicity was right. After all, what could possibly go amiss that an educated, industrious young woman couldn't handle?

Reggie seemed delighted to be once again taking a trip to Witcheston, though Major had a hard time of it with two more passengers to pull.

Ever conscious of the time slipping away, Meredith grew impatient with the elderly horse's plodding gait, but there was little she could do except pray they had time to visit the bank before it closed.

She couldn't escape the worry that her contact with Emma would be broken before she could bring her family's killer to justice. Everything rested on what she could achieve that morning, and time was of the essence.

Arriving at the Sandalwood Estate, both Felicity and Essie remarked on the grandeur of the house and surrounding grounds. The sprawling Georgian mansion, with its magnificent red brick portico and tiered lawns, was indeed a sight to behold. Driving past ornate ponds with gushing fountains, Essie exclaimed in delight, forgetting her anxiety in the pleasure of viewing such lush surroundings.

Reggie drew up at the foot of the wide steps and leapt down to help the ladies out of the carriage.

"We shan't be more than a few minutes," Meredith told him, "so don't wander too far away."

Reggie touched his cap with the tips of his fingers. "I'll just go for a short stroll, m'm. I'll be within earshot if you need me." He gave her a significant look, as if assuring her he would be there to come to her rescue if required.

Meredith sincerely hoped that wouldn't be necessary as she led the way up the steps and tugged on the bell rope.

Chester, the butler, opened the door, wearing the customary disdainful expression.

At first, Meredith thought he would refuse them entry when she asked to speak to Mrs. Pettigrew. After a moment's hesitation, however, he drew back and allowed them to enter.

Essie's gaze swept the grand hallway, then focused on the gleaming crystal chandelier with its intricately patterned gas shades. "Heavenly," she whispered.

Felicity seemed unimpressed and ill at ease. She kept glancing down the hallway to where the butler had disappeared. "Houses like this make me uncomfortable," she muttered. "Can't stand all this highfalutin nonsense."

"I think it's beautiful," Essie whispered, gazing in awe up the sweep of staircase soaring to the first floor. "I'd love to see it all."

"Then ask Will Barnard to show you," Meredith whispered.

Just then the butler returned, his nose tilted a shade higher. "Step this way, madam," he ordered, and proceeded to lead them to the same room where Meredith had met with Mrs. Pettigrew earlier.

The widow stood by the fireplace when they entered, and made no effort to come forward as the butler announced their names.

Meredith stepped forward and offered a smile. "I'm sorry to intrude on your morning," she said, "but my companions and I are seeking volunteers to help with the Christmas pageant at Bellehaven in December. We were wondering if you could oblige."

Mrs. Pettigrew flicked a glance at Essie and Felicity. "You are all teachers?"

Felicity answered. "We instruct future debutantes in cultural and social activities, yes." Her tone dared the woman to cast aspersions on such a noble cause.

"Is that so." The widow turned back to Meredith. "I admire your fortitude, Mrs. Llewellyn. It can't be easy soliciting volunteers for such an ambitious project. I'm afraid, however, that I'm unable to participate. I always spend the Christmas season in London. On the other hand, I can offer you some refreshments before you continue your search." She reached for the bell rope and tugged it. "And this time I insist. If you would all care to take a seat?"

Meredith would have preferred to do without refreshments, but she didn't want to risk offending the woman, and she still had to find a way for Essie to meet Will Barnard. "Thank you," she murmured, signaling to her friends to sit down, "you are most kind."

The refreshments, brought in by a smiling housekeeper, consisted of Welsh rarebits and custard tarts, a pot of tea, and a decanter of sherry.

Meredith waited for a decent interval in the conversation before asking, "If I might inquire, I wonder if your nephew might be willing to assist us with the pageant? Since we are mostly women in our establishment, it is difficult to find enough strong hands to work with the backdrops and scenery."

"We can certainly ask him." Once more Mrs. Pettigrew reached for the bell rope. "Though I must warn you, my nephew always has a full calendar over the Christmas season."

The poker-faced butler appeared and was dispatched to fetch Will Barnard.

Stealing a glance at Essie, Meredith noticed she had hardly touched the food on her plate. No doubt she was nervous again, now that her task was about to begin.

When Will Barnard entered, though, Essie seemed

pleasantly surprised. He, in turn, was most receptive to her charms, bending over her hand far longer than the brief touch Meredith and Felicity had received.

"These charming ladies wish to know if you would be willing to help them with their Christmas pageant," Mrs. Pettigrew announced as her nephew took a seat next to Essie.

Will looked at Essie, his eyebrows raised. "You teach at Bellehaven, Miss Pickard?"

"I do." She gave him her sweet smile. "You seem surprised, sir."

"I am. Most happily so." The look he gave her made her blush. "In that case, I shall be happy to be of assistance in any way I can."

"Splendid!" Felicity's hearty approval took them all by surprise. Especially so since her eyebrows worked up and down in an obvious signal to Essie.

Meredith hastened to attract Mrs. Pettigrew's attention away from her friend. "These are delicious tarts. So delicate in flavor."

"I am blessed with an excellent pastry cook." Mrs. Pettigrew reached for another tart. "She quite spoils me, I'm afraid." She gestured at the plate. "Do have another."

Meredith glanced at the clock. "I'm afraid we must take our leave shortly." She glanced at Essie, but the young woman's attention was fully focused on whatever Will Barnard was murmuring to her. Apparently she had forgotten they were pressed for time. Felicity seemed about ready to leap up any moment and say something outrageous to jog Essie's memory.

In desperation, Meredith said loudly, "I was telling Miss Pickard what a beautiful home you have. She was quite anxious to see it, weren't you, Miss Pickard."

Cheeks flushed, Essie started as if she'd been scalded. "Oh, yes, yes! It is just as lovely as Meredith described. I do so love majestic houses like this one."

"Then you shall see all of it." Will jumped to his feet. "Allow me to give you the grand tour."

Felicity let out her breath on an explosive sigh, while Meredith leaned back in relief.

Essie rose to her feet, smiling at Mrs. Pettigrew. "I do hope you won't mind?"

"Not at all." The widow glanced at her nephew. "Don't take too long, Will. These ladies are no doubt anxious to be on their way."

Meredith smiled at Will. "We do have another appointment, but I'm sure Miss Pickard will enjoy a *short* tour of your lovely home." She sent Essie a warning glance.

Looking worried now, Essie followed the young man out the door, while Meredith watched in growing concern. Until now she hadn't really thought things through. She had been so intent on getting answers that she hadn't considered the risk involved. If Will Barnard was guilty of setting the fire, Essie could be in real danger if he realized she suspected him.

Cursing herself for her lack of common sense, Meredith could only hope that Essie got the answers to her questions without arousing the young man's suspicions. All she could do now was pray Essie returned safe and sound.

Chapter 15

Although Meredith kept up a pretense of enjoying the conversation between herself and Mrs. Pettigrew, punctuated by an occasional comment from Felicity, she found it increasingly difficult to concentrate as the minutes ticked by.

Felicity kept glancing at the clock, which only intensified Meredith's discomfort. All sorts of sinister scenarios coursed through her mind as she murmured a vague *yes*, *no*, or *indubitably* in what she hoped were the right places.

Visions of Essie fleeing from a murderous Will Barnard, trapped in a corner fighting for her life, lying lifeless on the floor, tormented her . . . the last gave her such chills she actually shivered.

"You are cold?" Mrs. Pettigrew inquired. "I shall have Chester stoke up the fire." She glanced at the fireplace, where large chunks of coal glowed a fierce red.

"Oh, no," Meredith exclaimed, "I am quite warm, thank you. I was just wondering what is keeping Miss Pickard."

"I'm wondering the same thing," Felicity said grimly. "Perhaps I should see if I can find her."

She started to rise, but just then the door opened and Essie sailed in, laughing at something Will had said as he followed closely behind her.

Weak with relief, Meredith rather resented the fact that Essie appeared to be having such a good time while they'd sat so long worrying about her.

One look at Felicity's irate face, however, banished Essie's smile. She sent a guilty look at the clock. "Sorry. I didn't mean to take so long. Will . . . ah . . . Mr. Barnard was so very kind as to show me the gardens. They are absolutely divine."

"Thank you." Mrs. Pettigrew gave her nephew a rather stern look. "Perhaps you will show the ladies out, Will. I'm sure they are more than ready to be on their way."

Feeling remorseful, Meredith rose. Obviously her distraction had not been as inconspicuous as she'd hoped. "Thank you for your kind hospitality, Mrs. Pettigrew." She glanced at Will. Either Essie had failed to get answers from him, or the answers she had got had exonerated him from the crime. She couldn't wait to get outside and find out.

Will chatted with his vivacious companion all the way to the front door, and it was quite obvious they had taken to each other. Meredith hoped for Essie's sake that he'd been able to clear up any suspicions about his involvement in the Lewis fire.

They had barely reached the foot of the steps when Meredith could contain her curiosity no longer. Making sure the door was firmly closed behind them, she drew Essie to a halt. "Well? Did you ask him the questions?"

"I certainly did!" Essie's laughter floated up the steps. "I can't imagine how you could have suspected him of such a heinous crime. The man is utterly charming and such a gentleman. The time flew by so fast in his company. I was quite sorry for our tour to end."

"Oh, dear," Felicity muttered. "It appears we have an infatuation on our hands."

"Nonsense." Essie's cheeks grew pink. "I merely enjoyed his company, that's all."

Meredith felt like shaking her. "Well, what did he have to say?"

Essie danced down the last step and looked up at her. "Will was never in the Lewis home. He knew about the horses on the mantelpiece because his aunt gave them to George Lewis as a gift, after Mr. Lewis helped her with her finances."

Meredith let out her breath on a sigh. "And the gift to Will from his aunt?"

Essie turned away. "Ah, well, that was supposed to be a secret, but I managed to worm it out of him."

"Naturally," Felicity murmured.

Following Essie as she headed for the carriage, Meredith caught up with her. "What was the secret? Or did you promise not to divulge it?"

"No, I was careful not to do that." Essie halted once more. "Mrs. Pettigrew bought the headstones for the Lewis family's graves. She wanted it to be anonymous, and Will took care of the arrangements for her, without divulging who was responsible. She was so grateful she gave him the motor car, which had belonged to her husband."

Again Meredith puffed out her breath. "Well, that explains that. It appears that we can cross Mr. Barnard off our list."

"A short list, indeed," Felicity said. "That leaves only your bank manager, if I'm not mistaken."

"It does, indeed. We must make haste to reach the bank before it closes." Meredith hurried over to the carriage, where Major waited with his head down, his tail lazily flicking at the flies that landed on his back. Reggie was nowhere to be seen.

Meredith called out his name, and when there was no answer, Felicity cupped her mouth with both hands and bellowed, *"Reggie!"*

The sound of running footsteps answered and Reggie burst into view from around the corner of the mansion. "Coming! Coming!"

Essie and Felicity had already seated themselves by the

time he reached the carriage. His chest heaving in an effort to catch his breath, he got out a weak "Sorry. Fell asleep by the fountains."

"You need to get your proper rest at night." Meredith declined his hand and climbed up onto her seat. "Please hurry, Reggie. We must be at the bank in less than half an hour."

"Right you are, m'm." Still trying to recover his breath, Reggie saluted her, then leapt up onto his seat. Gathering up the reins, he shook them, shouted "Tally ho!" and they were off.

Being Saturday, Witcheston's High Street was less crowded than it had been on Meredith's previous visits. Reggie was able to pull up right outside the bank, and the three women alighted. Meredith gave instructions to Reggie to wait for them at the Pig and Whistle.

"I hope you all remember your parts," she said as Major clopped off down the street.

"I do," Essie said, still seemingly vitalized by her visit to the Sandalwood Estate.

"Of course you do," Felicity said gruffly. "After all, being able to charm gullible young men comes as second nature to you."

Essie seemed not to take offense. Instead, she gave Felicity a coy smile. "Be thankful that I am so accomplished at it, otherwise you might have to take my place."

"I'd rather be boiled alive." Felicity hunched her shoulders and stared at the door of the bank. "Let's hope we can do this without causing too much commotion."

"If we can't, then we are sunk." Meredith looked at Essie. "Give us no more than a moment or two. The bank will be closing in half an hour and we must be finished and out of there before then."

Essie nodded, then turned and sauntered down the street to the department store. Meredith waited just long enough to see her pause and stare at the window, then she beckoned to Felicity and hurried into the bank.

Desmond White was in his usual place, and Meredith

was relieved to see that he was alone behind the counter. Howard Clark wasn't due to return until late afternoon when the train arrived from London. All being well, they would have plenty of time to achieve their purpose.

Desmond recognized Meredith at once and called out to her. "Good morning, Mrs. Llewellyn. I shan't be more than a moment here." He finished serving the sole customer in the bank, an elderly man who seemed to take forever to finish his transactions.

At last he left, and Meredith approached the counter. She had barely opened her mouth to answer Desmond's greeting when Essie burst through the door in a high state of agitation.

"Oh, my, oh, my." Completely ignoring Meredith and Felicity, she stood wringing her hands and gazing at Desmond, despair written all over her lovely face.

Meredith felt quite impressed. She had no idea Essie was such an accomplished actress.

Desmond was obviously alarmed and anxious to oblige. He leaned forward, peering at Essie through the bars. "Can I help you, madam?"

"Oh, I hope so." Essie caught her breath on a sob. "It's my dog. My little Mitzie. She ran away and I can't find her!" She started sobbing, and her cries were so loud and heartbreaking that Meredith feared she was overplaying her role.

Desmond, it seemed, was quite taken in. He rushed to the end of the counter, lifted the flap, and hurried around the front to Essie. "Where did you see last see little Minnie?"

"Mitzie." Essie gulped.

"Pardon me. Mitzie."

"She was running down the street!" Essie pointed at the window and started that awful sobbing again.

Felicity made a slight noise and Meredith looked at her, afraid she would burst out laughing. Thankfully, Felicity merely turned her head and rolled her eyes.

Much to Meredith's relief, Desmond rose valiantly to the rescue. "What does Mitzie look like?"

Essie gulped out words between sobs. "She's . . . a . . . white . . . terrier. She's . . . wearing a . . . red . . . ribbon around . . . her neck!"

"Right! Got it!" Desmond turned around in a wild circle and flapped a hand at Meredith. "Can you keep an eye on things here until I get back? Just tell anyone who comes in I'll be right back." Before she could answer him, he tore out of the door and disappeared down the street.

Felicity exploded with laughter. "Essie, you were magnificent."

"Come," Meredith said, opening the flap on the counter. "We haven't a moment to lose. Essie, keep watch and let us know the minute you see Desmond coming in this direction. Then go out there and try to stall him as long as possible."

"I'll do my best." Essie wiped away the tears she'd squeezed out of her eyes and went to stand by the door.

Meredith held the flap open for Felicity, then let it drop behind her. "The door to Howard Clark's office is over here." She led the way, with Felicity hot on her heels. Pausing in front of it, she turned to her friend. "Can you unlock it?"

"There's not much I can't unlock," Felicity told her. She took a hairpin out of her hair and bent it into the required shape. "There weren't many advantages to being locked up in prison," she murmured as she bent over the lock, "but learning how to do this was certainly one of them. Comes in handy now and then."

Meredith was inclined to disagree. Felicity's prison sentence for protesting women's rights had been a terrible ordeal, and learning how to pick locks from an inmate could not possibly make up for everything she'd suffered at the hands of the prison guards.

"Ah, there it is." A click accompanied her words, and the door swung open.

Meredith slipped inside the room and Felicity followed, closing the door behind her. Crossing to the desk, Meredith went behind it and started pulling drawers open.

"The records are probably kept locked up," Felicity said, moving over to a large filing cabinet. "Let us hope they are not locked in a safe. They are a lot more difficult to open."

"But you could do it?" Meredith asked anxiously as she flipped open a ledger.

"If I had to, I suppose. But it would take longer. Ah, here we go."

Meredith glanced up to see the drawer to the file cabinet slide open. "Is it in there?"

"Wait a minute." Felicity leaned over the drawer, leafing through the files. "Wait . . . is this what you're looking for?" She pulled out a sheaf of papers and handed them to Meredith.

Taking them in both hands, Meredith eagerly examined the first page. "Ah! He didn't destroy them. I didn't think he would. He would have had to explain their absence at audit." Quickly she thumbed through them. "He was probably planning to alter the figures before they were examined by an auditor."

She put the papers down on the desk, her hands trembling with excitement. "It is here in black and white, signed by Howard Clark himself. The records clearly showing that he was responsible for embezzling funds from this bank and transferring them to his own account."

Felicity grinned in triumph. "Well done, Meredith. You have the scoundrel."

"For embezzling, at least. This will certainly clear George Lewis's name." She paused, staring at the papers. "I wonder if that will be enough for Emma."

"Let us hope so. What are you going to do about it?"

"These must be the papers George Lewis was planning to take to the inspector." Meredith gathered them up and folded them. Tucking them inside her coat, she added, "I will take them to the inspector myself. First thing on Monday morning."

"Good idea, I—" Felicity broke off as a loud rapping on the door was accompanied by Essie's urgent voice. "He's coming back!"

"Quickly, lock the cabinet again." Meredith slammed the drawer shut in the desk. "Come on, Felicity. We can't be caught in here." She rushed to the door and opened it, just in time to see Essie step outside. Luckily there were still no customers waiting at the counter, and she and Felicity were able to slip around the counter and replace the flap. Out on the street Essie's voice could be heard loudly urging Desmond to keep looking for Mitzie.

Reaching the door, Meredith opened it and looked outside. Desmond's hair was ruffled, and his cheeks burned from the effort of running back and forth. Her conscience pricking her, she called out, "Perhaps we can help the lady look for her dog!"

Desmond looked at her as if he would like to hug her. "Would you be so kind? I must get back to work or I'll be in trouble with my manager. He should be returning shortly."

"Of course we'll help." Felicity strode past Meredith and grasped Essie's arm. "Now, dear, why don't you show us where you last saw the little devil?"

Meredith nodded at Desmond. "I'll come back another day to finish my business here." She hurried off after the other two without giving Desmond time to answer.

Once out of earshot, both Essie and Felicity dissolved into laughter. "Poor man," Essie said, gasping in an attempt to control her mirth. "Did you see his face? I thought he was going to drop from exhaustion."

"Serves him right," Felicity said, recovering first. "He fell over himself to play the intrepid hero. I wonder if he would have been quite so eager had you been a man."

"Hush, you two." Meredith frowned at them both. "We took advantage of the fellow's good nature. I think it was most commendable of him to exert himself like that for the sake of a dog."

"Did you find what you were looking for?" Essie asked, finally sobering enough to speak calmly.

"I did, indeed." Meredith patted her coat. "The evidence to prove that Howard Clark, and not George Lewis, was the person embezzling funds from the bank."

Essie's forehead creased. "But how does that prove he set the fire in the Lewis home?"

"It doesn't," Meredith admitted. "I'm hoping that clearing her father's name will be enough to send Emma to wherever she needs to go."

Felicity gave her a keen glance. "You really don't know too much about this ghost business, do you."

"Nothing at all." Meredith sighed. "Which probably explains why I keep losing contact with them. It's so disconcerting."

"Well, you did manage to find the true embezzler," Essie reminded her. "You should be quite pleased about that."

"I'll feel much better once I have seen Emma again, and know that she'll be able to pass on. In the meantime, are you hungry? Reggie is waiting for us at the Pig and Whistle. The food there is excellent. They have a marvelous roast beef sandwich that is most satisfying." She started walking down the street in the direction of the pub.

Catching up with her, Felicity nudged her with her elbow. "I didn't know you frequented public houses."

"I don't. I just happened to have enjoyed a sandwich there the other day."

Essie uttered a shocked gasp. "By yourself?"

"No, actually I was accompanied by Reggie, and we sat outside in the beer garden to eat."

The look on Felicity's face was pure devilment, making Meredith heartily wish she hadn't mentioned her lunch with Reggie. "You and Reggie? That must have been an enlightening experience."

"I was hungry." Meredith quickened her step. "As I am now."

"Did you have a cocktail?"

"I had a glass of cider. Which I can thoroughly recommend."

Felicity chuckled. "Why, Meredith, I had no idea you were such a shameless reveler."

"I think a glass of cider sounds wonderful," Essie exclaimed.

"Then in that case, we shall all indulge." Felicity's long stride took her ahead of them. "Come, you slackers. Our cider awaits!"

Meredith had mentioned nothing to Reggie about the escapade they had planned that morning. He must have guessed something dubious was afoot, since he leapt to his feet when they approached the beer garden with a look of sheer relief on his face.

"There you are, ladies!" He doffed his cap and tucked it under his arm. "I was beginning to worry about you."

"Well, you can stop worrying." Meredith sat on one of the chairs and beckoned to the others to join her. "You can instead order roast beef sandwiches for the three of us, and three glasses of cider." She dug in her purse and pulled out some pound notes. "You may order for yourself as well."

"Well, thank you, m'm. Much obliged, m'm." Reggie sped away, and Meredith allowed her shoulders to relax. It had been an arduous morning, full of anticipation, anxiety, and confusion. Quite enough excitement for one day. She was ready now to return to the peaceful environment of Bellehaven House and enjoy a quiet afternoon in her room.

The sandwiches were devoured quickly, and the cider went a long way toward restoring Meredith's good spirits. By the time they had returned to the school, she was feeling quite optimistic about Emma's imminent reunion with her family.

The moment Meredith mounted the steps to the main door, however, it became apparent that all was not well within the hallowed halls of Bellehaven.

For one thing, a pair of lady's drawers hung from the gas lamp halfway up the stairs, and students were milling back and forth, some of them only half clothed, while a good deal of screaming and yelling echoed down the corridors to the point where Meredith had to cover her ears with her hands.

Behind her, Felicity let out a roar of outrage. "What the blue blazes is going on here?"

Essie shrieked as a heavy volume from an encyclopedia set hurtled over the banisters and crashed to the floor.

Meredith stared openmouthed at the chaos going on in front of her. What in heaven's name had happened while they were gone? Why were the students in a state of riot? Most important of all, where on earth was the woman she'd left in charge, Sylvia Montrose?

Chapter 16

Meredith grabbed the arm of a student and pulled her over to the door. Hustling her outside, she demanded, "Now, Andrea, perhaps you can tell me the meaning of all this bedlam?"

The girl's flushed face and bright eyes indicated she was in a high state of excitement. "We're rioting," she said, her voice shrill and high. "Against Miss Montrose."

Meredith raised her eyebrows. "What exactly did Miss Montrose do to deserve this horrendous behavior?"

"She's going to expel Sheelagh Radcliffe, miss."

Meredith wrinkled her brow. Radcliffe. A pretty girl with a daredevil attitude. The kind that easily got into trouble if not disciplined. She sighed. "What has Sheelagh done to cause Miss Montrose such aggravation?"

"She was in the closet, miss."

"In the closet?"

"Yes, miss. In the broom closet."

"What on earth was she doing in there?"

"She was with Mr. Platt, miss."

"Ah." Meredith was beginning to get a glimmer of the problem. "Perhaps you'd better start at the beginning."

Andrea took a deep breath. "Olivia lost the cross her mother gave her and asked some of us to help her find it and it sort of got to be a competition like a treasure hunt and everyone was running around and Miss Montrose was trying to stop us from running and then someone opened the closet door and there was Sheelagh with Mr. Platt and they were . . . doing something they oughtn't and Miss Montrose told Mr. Platt he would lose his job and then Sheelagh got really, really upset and told off Miss Montrose and Miss Montrose went berserk and told Sheelagh she was expelled from the school and some of the other girls started a protest just like the suffragettes do and . . ." She paused to take another deep breath, giving Meredith a chance to respond.

"I think I understand now, Andrea. I want you to go straight to your room and stay there until you hear the assembly bell. Immediately."

"Yes, miss." Andrea took one look at Meredith's expression and fled.

It took Meredith, Felicity, and Essie half an hour to get the students calmed down and safely confined to their rooms. Sylvia had locked herself in her room and Meredith spent another ten minutes talking her into opening the door.

Sylvia's version of what happened put her in a better light than had Andrea's account, but it was close enough that Meredith was satisfied she had the entire picture.

"We were extremely fortunate that Mr. Hamilton did not pay us a visit while all this was going on." Seated in Sylvia's impeccably clean and tidy room, Meredith gave her a stern look. "I don't have to tell you how displeased he would have been with the way you handled things."

Sylvia pouted. "There wasn't a thing I could do. The girls just took over everything. They were impossible to control. Nothing but a crowd of hooligans, in my considered opinion. What they are doing at a finishing school I have no idea. This establishment is a complete waste of time."

"The students behave perfectly well when suitably disciplined." Meredith stood. "I will let it go this time, but it's quite obvious you have a lot to learn about handling these young women. Most of them are spirited and even reckless at times, and will certainly take advantage of you if they sense a weakness. No matter what problems arise, you must never let them suspect that you are not fully in command of the situation. Whatever it takes. Do you understand?"

Sylvia's face was dark with resentment, but she nodded. "I will do my best."

"That's all we ask."

Stepping outside in the hallway, Meredith was relieved to find it empty and quiet. She decided to say nothing to Roger Platt. She would recount the incident to Stuart Hamilton on his next visit and let him deal with the wayward assistant. At least for now, peace had been restored to Bellehaven.

"It wasn't my fault!" Olivia crossed her arms and glared at Mrs. Wilkins. "I didn't ask them to go looking for my cross."

"If you hadn't lost it in the first place, none of this would have happened." The cook turned her back on the maid while she pulled a tray of scones out of the oven. "I hate to think what Miss Fingle is going to say when she gets wind of it."

"Well, maybe she won't hear about it if someone doesn't go blabbing about it to her."

Mrs. Wilkins straightened. "I won't say nothing, but she could hardly miss all that pandemonium that went on today. She'd have to be deaf not to hear all the row. Sooner or later she's going to get the whole story and then, my girl, you'll be in for it."

"It wasn't my fault!" Olivia looked at Grace for help. "Tell her it wasn't my fault. It was that stupid twerp, Mr. Platt, canoodling in the closet with that girl. That's what caused all the trouble."

"Well, it's not my place to say." Mrs. Wilkins tossed the scones onto a cooling rack. "You'll just have to wait and see what Miss Fingle has to say about it. Now go and get the tables ready for supper."

Grumbling under her breath, Olivia slunk out of the kitchen. Grace followed closely behind, feeling sorry for her. Nothing had gone right for Olivia this past day or two. Ever since she'd brought that wedding dress down from the attic.

"Stupid, stupid Mona," Olivia fumed as they marched down the corridor to the stairs. "What does she know about it, anyway? All she knows is what people tell her and she listens to the wrong people, that's all I can say."

Grace hurried to keep up with her friend. "Well, maybe no one will tell her how it got started. After all, Miss Montrose didn't get upset until she saw Mr. Platt and that girl."

"Yeah, well, it's just my bloomin' luck. I get the blame for everything around here lately." Reaching the stairs, Olivia started stomping up them.

"I keep telling you," Grace said, starting up the stairs behind her. "You should take that wedding dress back. It's brought you nothing but bad luck. Just like I said it would."

Olivia turned on her. "Oh, shut up about that flipping dress. I'm sick of hearing you bleating about it. It's got nothing to do with what happened and I'm not taking it back, so there!"

Her head still twisted in Grace's direction, she took another step, stumbled, and fell back. With a sharp cry, Grace went down with Olivia sprawled on top of her.

"Ouch!" Grace struggled to sit up.

"Now look what you made me do." Olivia got to her feet, then let out a shriek. Hopping on one foot, she made it to the stairs and sat down. "I think I've broken my ankle."

Grace scrambled up. "Oh, no. Let me look."

Olivia eased off her shoe. Underneath her black stocking her ankle was already showing signs of swelling. Staring at it in disgust, she muttered, "All right, Grace. P'raps you're right. I'll take the flipping wedding dress back to the attic."

Grace let out a sigh of relief. "I told you that dress was bad luck. I wonder who the bride was who wore it."

"Whoever she was," Olivia said grimly, "I'll be willing to bet she had a rotten marriage."

That night Meredith stayed awake for several hours hoping that Emma's ghost would return. When the child failed to appear the following night, Meredith awoke the next morning filled with worry.

She had looked forward to telling Emma she had cleared George Lewis's name, certain that it would be enough to send the little girl on to join her family. After giving it some thought, however, it occurred to her that Mr. Lewis's innocence had not been officially established, and wouldn't be until she had taken the evidence to the inspector.

As soon as her class ended that morning, she wasted no time in summoning Reggie and the carriage. Once more she found herself on her way to Witcheston, this time feeling a good deal more nervous.

Her dealings with the constabulary so far had been limited to a police constable by the name of Cyril Shipham— a rather unpleasant bully who made no secret of his utter contempt for women in general and the staff and students of Bellehaven in particular.

During her brief encounters with him, she had endured his insults only by an intense effort on her part to hold her temper. Therefore, she was not looking forward to dealing with his superior, who would quite possibly be even more detestable than the caustic constable.

Reggie seemed nervous when he pulled up outside the Witcheston constabulary and, after informing her he would be waiting at the Pig and Whistle, took off in great haste.

His behavior did nothing to settle Meredith's already fragile nerves. Carrying her canvas knitting bag, she entered the red brick building with a great deal of trepidation.

After waiting an intolerable amount of time, she was

ushered into an office by a dour police sergeant and left alone to wait for the inspector's arrival.

Seated in the stuffy room, she studied the walls, which were covered with various posters, notices, and a couple of official-looking certificates. She was squinting in an effort to read one of them when a tap on the door turned her head.

The door flew open, allowing a tall gentleman to enter. He appeared to be rather gaunt, as if he never had quite enough to eat. Thick black eyebrows emphasized the pallor of his face, and his grave expression pulled down the corners of his mouth.

It seemed to Meredith that Inspector Edward Dawson was not a happy man, though she wasn't quite sure why that idea had occurred to her.

He gave her a brief nod, then passed behind her to take a seat at his desk. Glancing briefly at a sheaf of papers in front of him, he pushed them aside, folded his hands in front of him, and regarded her with eyes that could have been either brown or green. "Mrs. Llewellyn. I believe you have something of importance to show me. My sergeant tells me you refused to leave it with him."

"Yes, I did." Meredith pulled the folded papers from her knitting bag. "I felt these should be delivered directly into your hands." She laid them on the desk and watched as the inspector picked them up with his long fingers.

"These appear to be some kind of bank records." He put them down and looked at her with a puzzled frown.

"I'm sure you are familiar with the house fire that killed a Witcheston bank manager, George Lewis, and his family a few weeks ago?"

Inspector Dawson's frown deepened. "Yes, I am, but—"

"Earlier that evening George Lewis had discovered evidence of an embezzlement. He made an appointment with you for the following day. I believe he intended to bring those papers to you himself."

"An embezzlement?" Still frowning, the inspector examined the ledger sheets.

"Yes, if you notice, the sum of the columns of figures

don't agree. Howard Clark, who is the current manager of the bank, filled out those ledgers and deliberately misrepresented the amount of money actually taken in for deposit. He kept the remainder of the money for himself. That is his signature at the bottom. I recognized it right away. He has a very distinctive signature. I saw it on papers he had on his desk when I visited him some time ago."

"I see." Dawson lifted his chin. "I shall be happy to look into this for you, Mrs. Llewellyn. You can safely leave them with me."

"Thank you, Inspector, but there's more. Much more." She pulled in a breath. "The day after George Lewis died, the embezzlement was discovered. Mr. Clark produced evidence that indicated Mr. Lewis had been the one responsible. Since I seriously doubt that Mr. Lewis intended to come to you with a confession of guilt, I believe that evidence had been fabricated."

After a moment's thought, Dawson nodded. "Looking at these records, I'm inclined to agree with you."

Encouraged, Meredith plunged on. "I also have reason to believe that since Mr. Lewis was on the point of bringing these papers to you, and when Howard Clark realized he was about to be arrested, he set fire to the Lewis home to silence Mr. Lewis."

One dark eyebrow lifted as the inspector gazed at Meredith. "That's quite an accusation."

"I have something else to show you." Delving into her knitting bag once more, Meredith produced the burned and twisted horse. Quickly she explained how she'd first seen it in the picture, and how she'd found it on the floor of the bedroom. She told him about Howard's spending, and his lying about being in London the day of the fire.

"My theory is that Mr. Clark used this horse to hit Mr. Lewis on the head while he slept," she said, "thus rendering him incapable. He may also have bludgeoned Mrs. Lewis before pouring lamp oil onto the bed and setting it on fire. Apparently he threw Mr. Lewis's pipe onto the bed as well, making it seem as if Mr. Lewis had fallen asleep while smoking it. Mr. Lewis's daughter, Emma, was in another room and managed to escape. Otherwise she would have perished in the fire as well."

For several seconds she endured the inspector's grave scrutiny, while she stewed inside, wondering what he was thinking.

Then, to her immense surprise and relief, Inspector Dawson smiled, revealing dimples that contrasted quite uniquely with the firm thrust of his jaw. "You must have given this a great deal of thought, Mrs. Llewellyn."

Meredith smiled back. "You have no idea."

"I must commend your remarkable initiative. I will certainly investigate the situation, though I must warn you, even if the Lewis family were victims of murder, there is no proof of the fact, and certainly no proof that Mr. Clark was the perpetrator."

Meredith sighed. "I was rather afraid you would say that. At least it could be proven that Mr. Clark is an embezzler, could it not? Thereby clearing Mr. Lewis's good name?"

"I believe that would be possible, yes." Dawson glanced down at the papers she'd given him. "I'll begin the investigation right away. I would imagine that Mr. Clark reported the embezzlement to his superiors, so I will have to get in touch with them."

"Thank you, Inspector. You have been most kind."

"Not at all, Mrs. Llewellyn. I thank you for bringing this to my attention."

He got to his feet and she rose with him. "You will let me know how it all transpires, I hope?"

Again he gave her a slow smile that she found quite pleasing. "It will be my pleasure, madam."

"Mine, too, Inspector." She allowed him to open the door for her, and bidding him good-bye, she left the building with a heart full of hope. She had officially cleared George Lewis's name. Now she fervently hoped Emma would make one last appearance so she could send her on her way and be done with the whole problem. It was time she got back to concentrating on her work.

That night Emma answered Meredith's prayers. Shortly after falling asleep, Meredith awoke to a cold room and a green mist hovering in the corner of the room.

"Emma!" She was wide awake instantly, fumbling for the oil lamp to get it lit before the ghost disappeared again. Peering at the shadowy figure, Meredith could barely make out the child's features. "Your father's name has been cleared. Soon everyone will know he wasn't an embezzler."

She wasn't sure what she was hoping for or expecting from the child. Somehow she felt sure she'd know when Emma passed on, just as she had known when dear Kathleen had left the earthly world for a better place.

This was different, however, for the ghost still hovered in the corner, as if waiting for something.

Feeling as if she'd failed the child, Meredith said quietly, "I'm sorry, Emma. I know you wanted me to find out who killed your family, and I believe I did. I just can't prove it. I only wish I could."

To her utter dismay, two ghostly hands reached out to her in mute appeal. For a second she could see Emma's face and the tears glistening on her cheeks. Then she vanished in a swirl of mist, and the room grew warm once more.

Meredith buried her head in her hands. She had failed after all. Emma was still trapped here on earth, and would be until her family's killer was brought to justice. She knew that now.

What was she to do? She had done everything she possibly could, even taking the case to Inspector Dawson. And he had told her there was no proof. What more could she do?

As if a voice answered her, the thought popped into her head. She could talk to Howard Clark's wife again. There had to be something, anything that would help her find the proof she needed to bring the man to justice.

Feeling only slightly comforted, Meredith slept.

It was late the next day before she could get away. Her classes had taken up most of the morning, and she had to attend the midday meal before she could leave.

Reggie chuckled as she climbed into the carriage that afternoon. "This is getting to be a regular habit," he said before he closed the door. "Old Major starts getting restless now if I don't get him harnessed. I think he looks forward to his jaunts."

"Well, don't get too used to it," Meredith said, settling herself on the leather seat. "Either of you. I'm hoping to get this over with very shortly, and then there will be no more of these trips."

Reggie gave her a sharp look. "You found out about the fire?"

"Yes, I did."

"So was it or wasn't it an accident?"

"As I told you, I don't think it was an accident, Reggie, but since I can't prove it, it's best not to discuss the problem."

"What about the bobbies? Do they know?"

"They know everything that I know, so I will have to leave the matter in their hands."

"Oh, so where are we going this afternoon, then?"

Reggie, she decided, asked entirely too many questions. "We are going to Mr. Clark's house again."

Reggie frowned. "Won't he be at the bank?"

"I'm going to talk to his wife. She's promised to help us with the Christmas pageant."

Reggie seemed to accept that, though he gave her an odd look before he closed the door.

Meredith felt guilty about misleading him, but on the other hand, she had no way of knowing if the visit would prove fruitful, and unless it was, there was no need for Reggie to know the real reason for calling on Sophie Clark.

Bowling along the narrow country lanes, Meredith prayed her meeting with the bank manager's wife would help her in some way. This was her very last chance to confirm her suspicions. If she failed now, all would be lost.

A guilty man would go free, and a lonely ghost would be doomed to wander alone forever.

Chapter 17

The bank manager's wife seemed happy to see her, and immediately ordered her housekeeper to provide tea and crumpets. While they were waiting for the food to arrive, Meredith brought up the subject of the pageant.

Sophie was obviously excited about the prospect, and Meredith felt a deep sense of remorse. If she was successful in bringing Howard Clark to justice, this poor woman would have to deal with the shame, and the loss of her husband.

It was with a heavy heart that she outlined the plans for the pageant. The housekeeper interrupted them, but once she had left the room, Sophie agreed to take charge of the costumes and declared that she knew just the person to make them.

"Vera is a wonderful seamstress," she said, touching Meredith's arm in her eagerness. "I'm sure she will be most happy to help."

"You are so kind." Meredith found it hard to meet the woman's eyes. "I do hope your husband won't mind you taking the time to help us."

Sophie shook her head. "Howard is far too busy with his work." She picked up her cup and saucer. "The bank means everything to him, you know. It's his life. I really don't know what he would do without it."

Meredith swallowed a bite of the buttery crumpet. "It must keep him busy."

"Oh, it does." Sophie took a sip of tea, then put the cup and saucer back down on the table. "I hardly see him, and when I do, all he can talk about is the bank business." Her laugh was a little forced. "I really don't understand a word he says, you know. I just nod and shake my head and hope it's in the right places. Not that he'd notice if it wasn't."

Obviously marriage to Howard Clark wasn't all fun and games, Meredith thought. Though it did little to make her feel better about the possible consequences of her visit. "He seems a very nice man," she murmured. "I've only met him once, of course. He was away the last time I went to the bank."

Sophie nodded. "I must say, he hasn't been quite the same since George died." She reached for the plate of crumpets and offered them to Meredith.

"No, thank you. I'll spoil my supper." Meredith smiled. "You were saying that your husband was affected by Mr. Lewis's death?"

"Oh, yes. Well, we all were, of course. It was such a terrible tragedy. But Howard seemed to take it harder than the rest of us." She bit into a crumpet and thoughtfully chewed for so long Meredith wanted to demand she finish what she was saying.

"I do hope he's feeling better now?"

Sophie seemed to have lost the thread of the conversation. She looked up with a vague expression. "Pardon? Oh, yes, I think he is, though he still has nightmares."

Meredith wasn't at all surprised to hear that, though it didn't seem as if this discussion was leading anywhere helpful. She was still trying to think of a way to ask the questions she wanted to ask, when Sophie spoke again.

"For a while there he was actually walking in his sleep."

She frowned. "Funny thing, that. He actually started do-ing it the very night George died. It was as if he had some kind of sixth sense about it."

Meredith sat up straight, her heart beginning to pound. This was it. Somehow she knew it. Very carefully, she put down her cup and saucer. "Your husband walks in his sleep?"

"Well, he did that night." Sophie shook her head. "I re-member, because we slept late the next morning and that's when we heard the news about George. I'd woken up in the middle of the night and Howard wasn't in bed. He wasn't anywhere in the house. I looked out of the window and there he was, walking up the garden path in his dressing gown and only one slipper on. Never did find the other one."

Meredith leaned forward, hardly able to contain her ex-citement. "It's a wonder he didn't wake up, walking on the gravel with a bare foot."

"That's what I thought." Sophie sighed. "At first I thought he'd taken ill, but when I went down to him and called out his name, he stopped and just stood there, his eyes tightly shut. I realized then that he was asleep. I led him back to bed and he never did remember anything about that night to this day."

"And you never found the other slipper," Meredith said, half to herself.

Sophie gave her an odd look. "No, we never did."

"How very strange." She was more or less talking to herself. A vision of the burned-out bedroom came to mind—the horse on the floor, a baby's scorched rattle . . . and one charred slipper.

Meredith drew a steadying breath. "Do you still have the other one?"

Sophie stared at her. "The other one what?"

"Your husband's other slipper."

"Well, I suppose I do somewhere . . . but why . . . what . . . I don't understand."

Realizing she had said entirely too much, Meredith got to her feet. "I'm terribly sorry, Mrs. Clark, but I really do have to go now. Thank you again for volunteering your services this Christmas. We shall look forward to your assistance." She had reached the door before the flustered woman could get to her feet. "Please, don't get up. I can see myself out." With that, she opened the door and hurried outside.

Reggie sat waiting for her with a bored expression on his face. "I thought all this traveling to and fro would be exciting," he grumbled as he climbed down from his perch. "But all I've done is mooch around while you have all the fun. I have more excitement looking after the water pipes in the school basement."

"I'm sorry, Reggie." Tense with anticipation, she looked up at him. "We have one more trip to make, then I hope this will all be over."

He studied her face. "You look as if you talked about more than the Christmas pageant."

"I did, Reggie. I certainly did. I think I have finally found a way to prove that my suspicions were correct."

"About the fire?"

"Yes, about the fire."

"It wasn't an accident?"

"No, Reggie, it wasn't."

"Who did it then?"

She shook her head. "I can't tell you right now."

"But you can prove it?"

"Yes, I think I can."

Reggie's face lit up. "Then what are we waiting for? Where do we go from here?"

She laughed. "Back to Bellehaven. I have to take care of a few things, and both you and Major need some refreshment. Give me an hour, then be ready to leave. We must get back to the school again before supper."

"Right you are, m'm!" Reggie leapt up to his perch and flicked the reins. "Tally ho, Major. We're on the track of a killer!"

Meredith winced. She would have to warn him not to

say anything to anyone about her planned trip. Until she had that slipper safely in her possession, the fewer people who knew about it, the better.

On her way to her office she passed Sylvia in the hallway. The young woman seemed ill at ease as she called out, "May I have a word with you, Meredith?"

Sighing, Meredith halted and reluctantly turned to face her. "I'm in rather a hurry—" she began, but Sylvia interrupted her.

"I shan't keep you a minute. I've had word that Mr. Hamilton will be calling around suppertime, and I was wondering if you intended to mention the incident with Mr. Platt."

Meredith puffed out her breath in frustration. The man's timing was as inconvenient as always. "I certainly intend to, Sylvia. I think Mr. Hamilton should be made aware of the facts."

"Yes, well, I was also wondering if you . . . if I . . ."

Realizing the source of Sylvia's concern, Meredith shook her head. "I see no reason to reveal your part in what happened. Mr. Hamilton doesn't have to know everything, does he."

Sylvia's face softened into a smile. "Thank you, Meredith. I am much obliged." She hurried off, while Meredith continued on her way, hoping fervently that Sylvia remembered her reprieve the next time she felt like tattling to Hamilton about something or other.

A little over an hour later she was ready to join Reggie in the forecourt. Major stood with his head down, and once more Meredith felt a stab of guilt for tiring out the poor old horse. She prayed that this would be the last time she'd have to drag the animal out on yet another jaunt when he was so tired and weary.

The journey to the Lewis home took longer than she remembered, and she was on pins and needles by the time she arrived. Ordering Reggie to stay with the carriage, much to his disgust, she made her way to the front door.

She was relieved to find the door was still unlocked. The idea of forcing her way into the house, even if it was abandoned and empty, was too unpleasant to contemplate.

Shuddering at the sight of the broken banisters, she thought about asking Reggie to accompany her. Once more she had been a little hasty in demanding he stay with the carriage.

Then she shook off her doubts. She would be but a moment or two, and then it would all be over. Very carefully, she began climbing the stairs.

The smell of burning seemed less overwhelming than the last time she was there, and she began to breathe a little easier as she mounted the steps to the landing.

A shiver ran down her back as she passed by Emma's room, but she stared straight ahead, her gaze fixed on the main bedroom door. She didn't want to think about the fear that poor child must have suffered.

With the floorboards creaking and cracking beneath her feet, she drew closer to the ravaged room. The smell was stronger now, and she wrinkled her nose as she stepped inside.

It looked much the same as when she'd last seen it—the remains of the bed, the baby's rattle, the scorched remains of the cradle . . . and the slipper. It sat just a few feet away, out of reach across the perilous charred floorboards.

Testing each step, Meredith edged closer and closer. The floor sagged beneath her weight, and she crouched on her heels to lean forward and grasp the edge of the blackened slipper. Drawing it toward her, she slowly shuffled backward, holding her breath as once more the floorboards sagged beneath her weight with an ominous groan.

She was afraid to turn her head to look behind her, in case the shift in weight shattered the flimsy remains of the floor. The journey back to the door seemed to be taking forever.

Out of the corner of her eye she saw she was almost level with the wall. Just a couple more inches and she would be relatively safe.

The harsh voice came out of nowhere, making her body jerk in shocked surprise.

"I do believe that belongs to me."

Forgetting to be cautious, she spun around. The loud crack seemed to echo around the room as her foot sank through the floor and was caught fast in the narrow gap.

"Well, now," Howard Clark said pleasantly, "I'll take that from you if you don't mind."

He stretched out his hand for the slipper, but with great presence of mind, she threw it as hard as she could across the room.

Struggling to pull her foot from the jagged hole in the floor, she muttered, "Go and get it, if you dare."

Howard Clark sighed. "It really doesn't matter. You're the only one who knows about it, and since you won't be talking to anyone about it, the slipper can sit there forever as far as I'm concerned."

Eyes widening, she stared at him. Surely he didn't mean what she thought he meant?

Howard's smile was pure evil. "Don't look so surprised, Mrs. Llewellyn. You really didn't expect me to simply allow you to walk out of here, did you?"

Frantically she renewed her efforts to drag her ankle free. The pain brought tears to her eyes, but she tugged all the harder, determined that this despicable creature would not get the better of her.

"It's such a shame." Howard stepped closer to her, pausing when the floorboards groaned again. "Here you were, rummaging through the remains of George Lewis's belongings for some obscure reason, when the floorboards gave way and down you went to the floor below. I'm quite sure you will be sorely missed by your students and friends."

With growing horror, Meredith saw him about to take another step toward her. "Wait!" If she could keep him talking long enough, maybe Reggie would be concerned enough to come looking for her again. How stupid she was to have walked in here alone. "How did you know I was here?"

Howard gave her another of his unpleasant smiles. "When I arrived home this afternoon, my wife informed me of your visit. She was confused by your great interest in one of my slippers. When she told me that she'd told you about my sleepwalking the night good old George died, I realized you had put everything together, and that the slipper must still be here. I had thought it was destroyed by the fire."

"So you came here to get it."

"Exactly. I had hoped to get here before you. Without the slipper, you would have had no way of proving that I had anything to do with the fire."

"You could have just destroyed the other one," Meredith pointed out. "Then I'd have had nothing with which to match this one."

"Ah, but had you shown that one to my wife, she would almost certainly have recognized it. She bought them for me, you see. Had my initials stamped right into the leather. I couldn't take the chance of those letters still being visible."

Meredith rocked her ankle from side to side in an effort to widen the gap. "So you killed Mr. Lewis to prevent him from reporting your embezzling."

"I had to. I would have lost everything—my job, my wife, my home, my entire life." Howard edged closer. Close enough to grab hold of her. She shrank away from him, and he sighed. "It's no use, Mrs. Llewellyn. You have to die. I can't let anyone know what I did."

He reached out his hands, and with a tremendous effort she dragged her foot free. Spinning away from him, she gave him an almighty shove, and he went sprawling across the floor.

At the same moment another pair of strong hands grabbed her from behind, hauling her backward as, with a roar of tearing carpet and splintering wood, the floor finally gave way.

Howard's scream echoed to the rafters, followed by a

deafening crash and clattering that seemed to go on and on, until finally, all was silent.

Trembling with shock, Meredith looked up into the grim face of Inspector Dawson. "Thank goodness," she said weakly. "I thought you'd never get here."

Seated in the teacher's lounge later, her bound ankle propped up on a footstool, Meredith smiled at the three faces regarding her with touching concern.

Essie had tears in her eyes, while Sylvia looked paler than usual, and even Felicity seemed shaken by the story Meredith had just related.

"You should never have gone there without us," Felicity said gruffly. "You came so close to dying out there all alone. Don't ever do that again."

"I wasn't exactly alone," Meredith said gently. "I rang Inspector Dawson before I left here, asking him to meet me there. I wanted him to be there when I found the slipper, so I could give it to him right away."

"He's rather good-looking," Essie said, clasping her hands together. "How romantic to be rescued by such an imposing gentleman."

Felicity sniffed. "Trust Essie to find something squishy in the midst of disaster."

Meredith smiled. "The inspector saved my life. I shall be indebted to him."

Sylvia leaned forward. "I'm so happy you survived that awful ordeal, Meredith. Though I'm sorry about your poor ankle. If there's anything I can do to help out, please let me know." She straightened. "I had better go to the dining hall. The students will be there for supper, and we are expecting Mr. Hamilton any minute." She glanced at Essie with a clear question on her face.

Essie nodded. "Yes, yes, we are coming." She touched Meredith's hand. "We shall see you after supper. Mrs. Wilkins will be bringing yours up here shortly. We thought it best, so you won't have to hobble to the dining hall."

"I appreciate that." Meredith wiggled her toes and grimaced. "It is rather painful."

Felicity patted her shoulder. "Well, you just sit there and enjoy the solitude. We can talk about all this later." She followed the other two out the door, leaving Meredith alone.

Leaning back in her chair, Meredith uttered a sigh. She felt weary, as if all the strength had been drained out of her. It was a satisfying feeling, though, to know she had achieved her purpose.

Now that she had finally put the matter of the Lewis family's murder to rest, she felt quite sure that she would see Emma no more, and that from now on she would be able to sleep peacefully. In fact, a little doze right now might help to regain her well-being. Snuggling down in the chair, she closed her eyes. She was about to drift off when the familiar chill crept over her. "Emma?" She had spoken the name before she opened her eyes, and to her delight a patch of mist hovered near the window.

Knowing she had little time before being disturbed, Meredith held out her hands to the ghostly figure swaying back and forth across the room.

"I did it, Emma. The horrid man who killed your family is dead. Your father's name is cleared and now you can rest in peace."

For an anxious moment or two she thought she had failed to communicate with the ghost, as the mist began to fade. Just as she was about to give up hope, the child's figure grew strong and she could see Emma's face. One ghostly hand rose to her mouth and she blew a kiss and then, for the first time, she smiled.

It was such a beautiful smile Meredith blinked back tears. Before she could utter another word, however, the mist swirled around the ghost, swallowing it up before fading away to nothing.

Meredith stared at the spot for several moments, then uttered a deep sigh. She would not see Emma again. She would miss her, but knowing the child was with her family was consolation enough. Closing her eyes, she drifted into a restful sleep.

The sound of the door opening woke her, and she sat up, staring at her visitor in surprise.

"Forgive me for disturbing you," Inspector Dawson said, "but I thought you might want to know the outcome of your little adventure this afternoon."

"Oh, yes, indeed." Embarrassed, she struggled to sit up. "I was wondering what happened to Howard Clark."

"Broke his neck in the fall, I'm afraid. Though it will save us from prosecuting him."

"Oh, dear." She felt a pang of dismay. "I suppose there are some who would say he deserved it, but I find it very troublesome that I caused a man's death."

"You did nothing of the sort." The inspector nodded at a chair. "May I?"

"Oh, please do."

He sat down, pressing his hands between his knees. "Mrs. Llewellyn, Howard Clark was an evil man, who had no compunction about killing an entire family in the most horrible way to save himself. He would have had no qualms about sending you to your death as well. He caused the fire that weakened the floor and, in so doing, precipitated his own demise. In no way should you feel remorse. Indeed, you helped bring a man to justice, and clear a good man's name in the process. I commend you for your persistence, though I have to admit, I'm at a loss as to what prompted you to take such risks."

She smiled. "I had my reasons. Thank you, Inspector. You have eased my mind."

"I'm glad. I wish I had arrived a little earlier to save you from injuring your foot. I did arrive in time, however, to overhear Howard Clark admit his evil crime. Had he not perished in the fall, I should certainly have arrested him for the murder of Mr. and Mrs. Lewis and their baby."

"And ultimately their daughter." Meredith sighed. "If it hadn't been for the fire, Emma Lewis might still be alive."

"Quite. All very sad." The inspector rose to his feet. "I must take my leave. I sincerely hope your injuries heal in a very short time."

"Thank you, Inspector."

To her astonishment, he reached for her hand and brought it to his lips. "I also hope we meet again, under more pleasurable circumstances in the future."

Without warning, from the doorway came the sound of someone clearing his throat. "Excuse me. I didn't mean to interrupt."

The inspector straightened, and Meredith looked past him to where Stuart Hamilton stood in the doorway, a decidedly frosty look in his dark eyes.

"Not at all, old chap." Inspector Dawson smiled down at her. "Farewell, Meredith. Until the next time."

Before Meredith could recover from his use of her Christian name, he had nodded at Hamilton and left the room.

Stuart Hamilton advanced toward her, his mouth drawn in a tight line. "I had no idea you were on first-name terms with the chief of the constabulary."

Nor had she, but she was not about to admit it. "Forgive me for not getting up," she said, "but I am somewhat impaired at the moment."

"So I see." He glanced down at her ankle. "How did that happen?

Meredith hesitated, knowing she could never admit the truth. Stuart Hamilton would never condone her dubious extracurricular activities while she was supposed to be educating the young women of Bellehaven. After all, hunting down a criminal was hardly setting a good example of ladylike behavior and decorum.

In fact, looking back on the events of the past week or so, it seemed as though quite a different person had occupied her body and mind—someone far removed from the stately headmistress of Bellehaven House.

And she rather liked her.

"I had no idea it was such a big secret."

Startled, she looked up to find Hamilton staring at her. Realizing she hadn't answered his question, she grew flustered, and frantically sought a reason for her injury that would sound feasible.

"Oh, it's no secret. I tripped on the stairs and wrenched my ankle. Rather clumsy of me, I'm afraid." Her laugh sounded false and she dropped her gaze.

After a long pause, Hamilton said lazily, "I trust the damage is not permanent?"

"Not at all. I shall be up and about in no time."

"Good." He looked at her for so long she again had to drop her gaze. "I'm glad to hear that, since I brought you a little present."

She looked up, just in time to catch a look in his eyes that further disturbed her composure. "A present? How very thoughtful of you."

"Yes, it's in the stable."

"Oh?" She frowned, wondering why he had chosen to leave it there, but fearing it too impolite to ask.

"If you insist on chasing all over town, you will soon put that ancient animal of yours in the ground. I believe you will find your new horse has a far stronger constitution."

It took her a moment to form words. "A new horse? That's truly wonderful! Thank you so much, Mr. Hamilton."

"My pleasure." He nodded, and began to move away. "Take care of that ankle. We don't want you injuring it further. Stay off it as much as possible. I'll send Dr. Mitchell to take a look at it in a couple of days."

"That's very kind of you."

"Not at all." He got almost to the door, hesitated, then came back to her. Reaching for her hand, he muttered, "What's good for the goose is good for the gander." Raising her hand, he touched her fingers with his lips. "Until next time, Meredith."

Speechless, she watched him leave. Only then did she

remember she had forgotten to report Mr. Platt's indiscretion. Her skin still tingling from the contact of her fingers with Stuart Hamilton's mouth, she smiled.

Perhaps she should simply forget her assistant's deplorable behavior for now. After all, it seemed an excellent time for second chances. For all of them.